MISSOURI AVENGER

The war was over and Reconstruction had taken over the country. Southerners suffered badly at the hands of some Yankee regulators, but Deke Hardy didn't aim to be one of them. He was warned that he didn't know what he was doing, taking on someone like Colonel Kyle O'Connor, the Reconstruction Controller in Hardy's neck of the woods. But they got it wrong: it was O'Connor who didn't realize what he was doing taking on Deke Hardy . . .

Books by Clayton Nash
in the Linford Western Library:

DAKOTA WOLF
LONG-RIDING MAN
THE MUSTANG STRIP
BRAZOS STATION
DIE LIKE A MAN

CLAYTON NASH

MISSOURI AVENGER

Complete and Unabridged

LINFORD
Leicester

First published in Great Britain in 2000 by
Robert Hale Limited
London

First Linford Edition
published 2002
by arrangement with
Robert Hale Limited
London

British Library CIP Data

Nash, Clayton
    Missouri avenger.—Large print ed.—
    Linford western library
    1. Western stories
    2. Large type books
    I. Title
    823.9'14 [F]

    ISBN 0–7089–9805–4

Published by
F. A. Thorpe (Publishing)
Anstey, Leicestershire

Set by Words & Graphics Ltd.
Anstey, Leicestershire
Printed and bound in Great Britain by
T. J. International Ltd., Padstow, Cornwall

1

New Order

They had started out with 300-plus steers in Texas, driven them through the outskirts of the Indian Territory, fighting off renegades left over from the war as well as Indians, hazed and punched the beasts through storm and flood, and now — *now*, they were within spitting-distance of their destination, almost home.

For trail boss Deke Hardy, it was good to be back in Missouri and he was trying to absorb the *feel* of the land, the plains and the rivers and forests and the rugged hills they were heading for.

It was years since he had been back here, *long* years that he would just as soon forget.

And then he saw the line of armed Yankees stretched out clear across the canyon entrance, blocking the way.

Hardy was riding point with Flap-jack. He swore quietly as he held up a hand and the ragged riders in their remnants of uniform and old clothes did their best to bring the remaining 200 trail-weary steers to a halt. Young Johnny McGivern rode up, looking worried as usual behind the scar-twisted lift to one side of his mouth that gave him a permanent half-smile. A Yankee ball had done that to him at Manassas and his right hand was now resting on the worn butt of the old Griswald and Gunnison six-gun rammed into the length of rope that held his oversized trousers around his narrow waist.

'What they want, Deke?'

'Us — and the cows. We're in Reconstruction territory now, Johnny.'

Flapjack, a hard, sixtyish rider from somewhere west of the Pecos, spat. 'I've had me a bellyful of Yankees.'

That was all, but it voiced the general opinion of the seven-man trail crew, including Hardy. He signed to the others to wait, kneed his brown mount forward, one hand held at shoulder-level, palm out.

'Howdy, gents. We want to drive our herd through the canyon.' He addressed the officer, a rugged-faced lieutenant who had likely seen action in most major battles of the war. 'So, if you could have your men just move to one side, Lieutenant . . . '

'Throw down your guns and dismount and keep your hands high,' the officer replied in a deep voice, hands still folded on his saddle horn. 'You're goddamn Rebs and you're carryin' firearms, which you know damn well is agin Reconstruction law. You're in trouble, feller — a lot of trouble, but maybe there could be a way out for you . . . ' He paused as if thinking over some way to help. 'Like, say if you was drivin' them beeves up specially for our use.'

He hitched just a little in saddle, swinging his eyes along the line of his

3

men with their rifles gleaming in the hot Missouri sun and his mouth twitched. Most of his men laughed out loud. The officer swung his brittle gaze back to Hardy.

'That was what you was doin', wasn't it? Bringin' the conquerin' army plenty of beef . . . '

'You've got it wrong, Lieutenant,' Hardy said casually, using his heels to make his horse move skittishly as if it was nervous about something — and moving a little closer to the side. 'These cattle are for my ranch outside of Hardyville. We rounded 'em up in south-east Texas, drove 'em all the way here. If there're taxes to be paid on 'em, I'll pay, but I keep the cows. And my crew.'

The officer shook his head slowly. 'Well, I'll be a son of a bitch! You goddamn Rebs just don't know when you're licked, do you! War's been over for more'n a year and still you sass a Union officer . . . Men, I guess we just gotta take these beeves in for inspection and tax assessment. And we do it right *now*!'

Hardy wheeled his mount, snatching his big Colt Dragoon pistol from his belt as he did so. The Yankee rifles cocked and the lieutenant brought up his pistol and fired, the ball passing close by Hardy as he jumped his mount back towards the herd where his men were already moving. He triggered the Dragoon and the lieutenant slammed backwards over his mount's rump as if kicked by a giant mule. The Dragoon thundered again and the next man pitched sideways into the soldier next to him. Their rifles discharged as the rest of the troop fired into the trail men.

Two went down and Hardy, now back level with the stirring, bawling cattle, yelled, 'Stampede 'em! And then it's every man for himself!'

He blasted his gun close to the ear of one of the lead steers and the animal bawled, raked with his horns, catching the brown horse across the chest, as it lunged into the steer next to it. By now others were spooked and they were pressing from behind and suddenly the trail-worn herd came to life, bursting forward like a living flood — straight for the line of Yankee soldiers.

Some were still firing, but most took one look at the herd charging towards them and forgot about bringing down the trail men, whirled their mounts and started back up the canyon. The cattle were bawling, filling the canyon with a sound from hell, mixed with the drumming thunder of the hooves and the roiling dust now filling the canyon wall to wall, and the clashing of those murderous horns . . .

Hardy was yelling like a crazy Apache, having emptied his big gun. He leaned from the saddle, hit a cow behind the ear just to spur it on. The brown was faltering, blood spilling from the horn gash in its chest. He wheeled away as Johnny McGivern let out a wild cry as his horse stumbled and he was thrown into the edge of the herd.

Hardy spurred his horse forward but

it was too late — both McGivern and his mount had been trampled by the maddened steers.

Hardy wheeled away, hauling his wounded brown against the wall at the entrance to the canyon as the cattle surged through in an unstoppable river of death. He glimpsed bloody and torn Yankee tunics here and there, stood in the stirrups, looking for his men. They had taken him at his word — it was every man for himself. They were all making some kind of effort to escape, those still in the saddle.

Hardy wheeled the gasping horse, looking for somewhere he could pause long enough to examine the wound, and then he saw a horse coming out of the dust, eyes white and rolling, ears laid back, teeth bared with the bit between them. The rider had been shot out of the saddle or unhorsed by a lunge from a wild-eyed steer apparently, for he was now being dragged and bounced alongside the flying hooves, his Union blue uniform beginning to shred on his upper body. He had lost his hat and bright red hair flashed like a handful of fire. He saw Hardy, and the Reb hauled rein and began to stand in his stirrups in astonishment as he realized the man held a pistol in one hand, likely going to shoot the horse before he was dragged to death.

Instead, he shot Deke Hardy.

The redhead fired across his jolting body and it must have been pure luck that the ball sped true, but Hardy only thought about that later.

At the moment the gun fired, there was no time to think at all.

He dropped back into the saddle, spurs going back to rake the flanks of the wounded brown, and then suddenly there was a hammer blow alongside his right ear and there was a brilliant flare of white flame accompanied by a sensation of flying — briefly — before there was a sickening plunge, a smashing blow that jarred his whole being and then — nothing.

★   ★   ★

He didn't know where he was at first, only that he had a headache that felt like a bayonet had been driven in between his eyes. Lifting a hand in the darkness, he touched a tight bandage, a little damp in one place, wrapped firmly around his head.

Then he remembered the red-haired Yankee being dragged by his horse and the flash of the pistol. After that — *nothing*. Until now.

He had just discovered he was lying on a layer of musty straw against a rough stone wall, when a door slammed open and he recoiled from bright sunlight streaming in and slashing at his eyes. Two armed men came in and without a word grabbed him by the arms, hauling him roughly to his feet and propelling him out through the doorway.

He stumbled to one knee, saw that he was in a narrow, dank passage and then the guards hauled him upright again and shoved and butted him along the passage, up a set of slippery steps and through another doorway. This time the passage was built of paint-peeling timber and the steps to the floor above were wooden and he knew where he was.

City Hall, Springfield, Missouri.

Headquarters of the Reconstruction Administration for that state.

Past cubicle-like offices with closed doors, bedraggled folk waited — sullen and discouraged — on hard wooden forms against the walls at intervals. He saw at least two hollow-eyed men glance up and start when they recognized him. Hoarse whispers:

'Christ, it's Hardy!'

'What's that son of a bitch doin' showin' his face around here?'

'Didn't think he'd have the nerve!'

The rifle butt of one of the guards dropped painfully on to the dirty bare toes of this last speaker and the man howled as he quickly grabbed his throbbing foot.

Hardy heard no more whispers after that as he was taken to the end of a passage where a uniformed lieutenant sat behind a low varnished fence rail at a desk. Several soldier-clerks worked over papers behind him. The man stood.

'He's to be taken in at once,' he said, coming out through a gate in the rail and hurrying on ahead to a heavy varnished and panelled door with a polished brass handle. He rapped a knuckle on a panel, opened the door and looked in.

'The wounded Reb is here, Colonel,' he said.

Apparently receiving some kind of signal from inside he stepped back, holding open the door, jerking his head. The guards dragged Hardy inside the office and he heard the door close behind him. The guards stood at attention either side of him as they stopped him a few feet from a large desk cluttered with scattered papers. Behind it, easing back now in a high-backed, padded leather chair, was a thick-bodied man in a clean and pressed uniform, sporting colonel's insignia. He had a stern, roundish face with a hard mouth and cold-looking eyes, but he was handsome enough with an abundance of black tousled hair curling down on to his forehead.

He was starting to press the finger-tips of his big hands together, the cold grey eyes raking Hardy from head to foot, when he paused, frowned, and suddenly sat up straight, leaning slightly forward as he inspected Hardy more closely.

He saw a tall man with wide shoulders, lean in the gut and hip-section, worn and trail-dusted range clothes covering the big frame. The face was hawk-lean, eyes green, the long, unkempt hair fair where it showed above the blood-spotted bandage wound about his head. He was unshaven — maybe three, four days' growth on his jowls — and the mouth seemed a little thin-lipped and hard.

The jaw was square and stubborn and Colonel Kyle O'Connor, Controller of the Reconstruction, for southern Missouri, knew this man would give a lot of trouble, especially if forced to do something he didn't want to.

'My hat, you've changed in some ways, Deke, but I recognize that stubborn jaw! It's a dead giveaway!' He was standing now, coming around the desk, ignoring the guards who were staring at him as he stopped in front of Hardy, signed to the soldiers to release his arms, then snapped, 'Get him a chair!'

The men stumbled into each other in their hurry to obey but a round-backed chair with a leather cushion was brought from against the wall and Hardy sank into it gratefully.

'Get out,' O'Connor told the guards and watched as they hurried to obey. As the door clicked closed, he smiled down at Hardy, thrusting out his right hand. 'Good to see you again, Deke. Must say I wasn't expecting it, but it's

13

good just the same.'

Hardy gripped with the man briefly, looking up awkwardly, his whole neck and shoulder region stiff.

'You've come up in the world, Kyle.'

O'Connor shrugged his heavy shoulders as he leaned his big hips against the front edge of his desk, folding his arms. 'Promoted on the field of battle — that's the way the citations read.'

Hardy smiled faintly. 'Guess you ain't changed much after all — you always did like to blow your own trumpet.'

For a moment, the Yankee's face hardened and the eyes closed down. Then abruptly he smiled, shaking his head slowly.

'Same goes for you. You look like hell and you're in more trouble than you can shake a stick at, and still you sass me in my own office!' He waited but Hardy said nothing. Suddenly, O'Connor snapped his fingers. 'My hat! *Hardyville*! I never made the association! It's named after your family, right?'

'My grandpa first settled there with a trading post. My pa and his brothers started a ranch and a small freight line and someone dubbed the whole she-bang Hardyville one day and it stuck . . . ' Hardy's voice took on a tenseness suddenly. 'Is it still standing?'

'Mostly — it didn't suffer too badly in the war. I've had some cause to, er, demonstrate just how serious the Union is about Reconstruction, however, once or twice. The lesson seemed to be learned quickly enough.'

Hardy's green eyes were drilling into the colonel's face now. 'My family?'

'As I said, I didn't make the connection before, but as far as I know there is a young woman and a crippled boy living out there some-where . . . '

Hardy's hands were white-knuckled against the chair arms. 'A *crippled* boy?'

'So I believe — eighteen or nineteen, I think. I'd have to check the file. The woman is his sister . . . ' He arched his thick black eyebrows. '*Your* sister?

Which, of course, would make the boy your — '

'Kid brother, Larry,' Hardy said tightly. 'My sister is called Lee . . . '

O'Connor nodded. 'Yes, I believe that's the name.' He straightened, clapped his hands once as he went around the desk and dropped into his chair heavily, watching Hardy carefully. 'So, you have family surviving — I don't know what happened to the rest of your kin. Oh, wait! I think your . . . father, yes, it must have been him . . . Just as the war was about to end, some of our men required billeting and feeding for the night but this man Hardy refused to co-operate and, in fact, tried to shoot the officer in charge. Naturally, he was overpowered and — well, you know how strict a conquering army has to be in such cases, Deke.'

'You hanged him.' Hardy's voice was barely audible.

'I'm sorry, but war is . . . well, war.'

Hardy said nothing, but there was a

strange flintiness about his green eyes that turned them almost grey. They did not waver from O'Connor's face and the man flushed slightly, sat back in his chair and cleared his throat.

'Now, the war — or its end — has brought *us* together again . . . and you, too, have transgressed, killed some of my men. What shall I do with you, Deke?'

The grey-green eyes bored harder into O'Connor's face. 'Hang me?'

The Yankee smiled abruptly. 'My hat, *no*! Hang a man of your talents?' He shook his big head emphatically. 'No, sir — not when I can use those talents to make my job easier.'

Hardy tensed. 'If you think I'll help you — '

'Yes, that's *exactly* what I think, Deke!' O'Connor stood again, walked restlessly across the room and back, stopped by an ornately carved sideboy that Hardy recollected the citizens of Springfield had bought and paid for out of their own pockets for his Uncle Zack who had, at the time, been mayor of the town. The Yankee poured two stiff whiskies and brought one across to Hardy.

'Too proud to drink Yankee whiskey, Deke?'

Hardy took the glass and sipped, smiled faintly as he glanced up. 'Genuine Tennessee bourbon, Kyle — Yankee only by way of looting I'd say.'

O'Connor scowled. 'Well, remember that. It's the right of a conqueror to pillage and plunder.'

'Kyle, you're making the same mistake all of you Yankees do — the South hasn't been conquered. Just worn-down. We might've *lost* the war, but that don't mean the North *won*. Not by a damn sight.'

'All right, all right. We won't sit here arguing over terminology. This is Reconstruction and it's my job to see it's implemented according to the Act to the best of my ability — and that is what I aim to do.' He sipped some of his whiskey but his face gave no hint as to whether he enjoyed it. 'Deke, you can be a big help to me, just as I can be to you. It comes down to a simple choice, really: you help me so that things run smoothly around here and your people cause me a minimum of trouble, or you can refuse. And I'll hang you for murder.' Smiling, he lifted his glass in a brief toast. 'Welcome home, Deke . . . welcome home! To the New Order!'

2

Decision

There it was — only a blur on the horizon right now, but a welcome sight anyway. For a long time, he had thought he would never see it again.

Hardyville, West Missouri.

Not much of a town, more like what he had heard called a 'hamlet' when he had been up north, but it bore the family name and for many years it had worn it with honour, if not a certain amount of pride.

Of course, that might not be the case now: not with the stories that had circulated about him.

He set his horse towards the scattered buildings, riding slowly, maybe subconsciously delaying the moment when he would appear again on the main street. The horse was a powerful

20

black, supplied by Colonel O'Connor. Hardy had tried to push his luck and asked for firearms, too, but the Controller wouldn't go that far.

'Daren't do it, Deke. It's written law that no Southerner can carry a firearm without special permission and it has to be a damn strong reason at that.'

'Well, if I'm gonna be working for you . . . ' Hardy had tried tentatively, one last time, knowing the answer, so he wasn't surprised when O'Connor had shaken his head emphatically.

'I'll send along Sergeant Field for your protection if you think you need it.'

Hardy curled a lip wryly. 'And who protects me from Sergeant Field?'

That brought a chuckle from the colonel. Field was the redhead who had shot Hardy out of the saddle while being dragged by his horse. Apparently he had gotten himself free without major injury and had been the man to actually bring Hardy in as prisoner. He was one tough Yankee and had no liking for anything remotely connected with the South.

He rode a little behind Hardy now as they closed on Hardyville, eyes alert, showing no real concern, confident in his position as a member of the conquering army that he could handle any trouble that might come his way.

Hardy hadn't planned on even giving O'Connor a hearing when the man had first suggested he help smooth the way for the implementation of Reconstruction Law. But O'Connor had pressed on regardless and, despite himself, Hardy had found himself not only paying attention to the man, but even beginning to give consideration to the idea.

'Look, Deke, it's a long time since you scouted and trail-blazed for the army in Dakota. You had rank equivalent to a lieutenant even though your status was considered to be civilian. We rode a lot of trails together, fought side by side against Indians and renegade whites and shared grub and tobacco on more than one occasion.'

'Still didn't make us friends,' Hardy cut in.

O'Connor arched his eyebrows. 'Oh? I think I regarded you as a friend, Deke, in those days — anyway, we were comrades in arms, if you prefer it that way. You were leading some gold or silver escort in Idaho, as I recall, when war finally broke out . . . ' The colonel leaned forward across his desk. 'I heard you stayed there in that damn territory that couldn't make up its mind whether to fight or not — or on which side. In fact, I heard you took no part in the war at all.'

Hardy wasn't going to answer, then changed his mind. 'Didn't seem to be any of my business. We'd never run slaves back home in Missouri. We'd helped a couple of runaways now and again, but at another time when the runaway had left his boss's family chopped-up and spread around the countryside, including two children, we strung him up from the nearest tree.'

He shook his head. 'No, the war had nothing to do with me. I was interested in helping open up the country for settlement and I couldn't see that the North and South tearing each other's throats out was going to do anything for that.'

O'Connor tapped his large fingers gently against his desk. 'That could be construed as a form of treason . . . '

Hardy shrugged. 'That's the way it was. In Idaho, I guess I helped both sides on occasion when they appeared and needed guiding into wild country.'

'Hmm. I did hear some rumours that you worked undercover for the South, but — that's past. War's over and if you're truly interested in seeing the peace last and want to help bring about some order out of the chaos that exists, you'll listen to me — and help me. What do you say, Deke?'

'I say, what do you have in mind?'

'Ah! That's more promising than I'd hoped. Very well, just listen without interruption and I'll explain . . . '

Hardy had intended to drift with his own thoughts while the Yankee put forward his ideas, but he found himself paying more and more attention, and by the time O'Connor was finished, he was thinking that some of those ideas made pretty good sense.

Naturally, there had been resistance to the Reconstruction and the brutal treatment of the soldiers who administered its laws. O'Connor made no bones about how rough he had had to be to show the Missourians that he meant business: he was bringing a new order to this neck of the woods and by God he *would* have obedience and a measure of respect or there would be Rebs dangling from every tree for miles around.

Hardy listened, tight-lipped, under the grave stare of the Controller. He didn't like what he heard, but he savvied it.

'Your town, Hardyville, has given me very much more than token resistance, Deke. In fact, I've had to come down hard on the people who refused to toe the line, but even though you never actually served in the army, you know that there's always a higher-up and he passes orders down the line and if the men under him know what's good for themselves, they obey those orders.'

Excuses, thought Hardy. Then said aloud, 'I know. But I also know there's a certain amount of . . . interpretation of any order given. Just how it's carried out is often up to the man doing it.'

O'Connor held up one big hand. 'This is Reconstruction, Deke. Like it or not, we are the conquering army. It's always been rough on the losers. Bad things happen and that's just the way it is — I make no apologies. I've a damned difficult job to do and I get it done any way I can — which is why I'm trying to recruit you to help me bring peace to this neck of the woods.' The Yankee smiled thinly. 'There'll be a suitable reward, of course.'

'Do I get to pick it?'

The colonel laughed briefly, shaking

his head slowly. 'You *are* a hard one! Well, perhaps we'll see, anyway. Meantime, I have to confiscate your cattle that survived the stampede.'

Hardy's eyes narrowed. 'I was hoping to take at least a hundred out to the ranch for the family . . . '

O'Connor kept shaking his head. 'Out of the question, I'm afraid. I have a lot of men under my command and they all have to be fed.' He twisted his mouth. 'The folk around here don't see fit to supply us with sufficient food so we simply have to take it by force. But your cattle will ease that burden for a time . . . '

Hardy didn't pursue it. 'How about my men?'

O'Connor lifted his big hands and spread them. 'All killed in the stampede, or the fight with my soldiers afterwards. You were the only survivor.'

That hit Hardy, but apart from a brief silence, he didn't react.

'I need time to think it over.'

'I'll give you till morning.' The Yankee

leaned across the desk, his gaze steady on Hardy's rugged face. 'I want you with me, Deke, because I believe together we can bring order out of chaos much more quickly and even pleasantly, but I'm not going to beg you. But think of this: if you accept, I'm willing to write my report about an accidental stampede that killed some of my men in that canyon. It may not be too palatable to some, but I have enough authority to see it passed through. However, if you refuse, you'll be dangling from our hanging tree by sundown tomorrow . . . '

The decision, of course, wasn't hard to make: Hardy wasn't about to swing at the end of a rope if it could be avoided. Besides he needed to see Lee and his kid brother, Larry. Had to see them right, no matter what it took. He knew the folk of Hardyville had likely heard stories about him not fighting in the war and they would resent it because almost all the menfolk had joined the Confederacy.

Some would label him coward and they wouldn't whisper it, either . . . but just maybe he could save a few lives.

That was a bridge to cross when he came to it. But, for now, he agreed to help O'Connor and here he was, riding in on the scattered buildings of his home town with the hard-eyed, red-haired sergeant, Brick Field, at his stirrup, right hand never far from the butt of the holstered Remington Army pistol at his belt.

In a very few minutes, he would find out what kind of a reception he was going to get.

★ ★ ★

Main Street was never big nor was it even a good-looking street, but now — well, Hardy couldn't believe how dingy and mean it was. The buildings were all in need of paint or repair or both. The gutters meandered as if some drunken farmer had stumbled along behind his plough and decided to let the horse drag it where it would. There were pot holes filled with scummy water and garbage was scattered about.

There were folk on the broken boardwalks, too. Hunched-over folk with shifty eyes, drab clothes, some cringing and hurriedly stepping aside when uniformed Reconstruction soldiers came towards them. Some of the soldiers were obviously drunk, others hung-over. A couple of painted women hung on the arms of three privates as they weaved down the middle of the street, singing bawdily.

'Must feel good to be back, huh, Reb?' said Brick Field with a slight sneer.

Hardy did no more than throw him a cold look, searching for a familiar face amongst the people. Before he located one, he heard a voice out of the past from his left and behind him.

'Hey, folks!' it bawled harshly. 'Will you just goddamned look at what's had the goddamn gall to turn up here — *and* in the company of one of them

Yankee scum! It's l'il ol' Deacon Hardy hisself. Recognized him by that big yaller streak down his back!'

As Hardy began to turn in the saddle, Field cursed and dragged at his pistol. 'That 'scum's' gonna cost you plenty, Reb!'

Hardy grabbed the man's thick wrist and their eyes clashed as the sergeant strained to bring up the gun.

'Leave it, Brick! It's me he's insulting.'

'Mebbe you don't hear good!'

Field was unable to break Hardy's grip and finally he let the gun drop back into the scuffed army-issue holster. But his pale eyes blazed as finally Hardy turned to look at the man who had shouted.

His name was Dal Gilbert and he had one arm less than the last time Hardy had seen him. There were scars on the left side of his face, livid and disfiguring, the same side as the missing arm. It looked like he had less than a whole ear as well and hair hadn't grown properly on that side of his head, but Dal had made some effort to comb the longer strands across so as to hide the bare, twisted skin.

He was a man in his mid-thirties, Hardy knew, about his own age, but Dal Gilbert looked like a man of fifty. Lean as a rail, stoop-shouldered, bitter-mouthed, and dressed in patched bib-and-brace coveralls that were too short in the leg. His boots were bound with strips of rawhide that were almost worn through.

A frayed Confederate cap with a broken bill sat on the back of his head. Well, thought Hardy, Dal had always been a stubborn cuss, never knew when to give up in any kind of a fight.

'Howdy, Dal. Good to see you again.' Hardy nudged his mount forward, leaned down a little as he thrust out his right hand.

Gilbert was as quick as a snake. His right hand snatched Hardy's and yanked him out of the saddle. He hit the street and Gilbert stepped in and kicked him in the chest. Hardy rolled and Gilbert came in stomping, cursing, a little spittle flying. Some men on the walks, including Yankee soldiers — cheered him on. Any kind of a fight was worth some attention in this hell-hole of a town under Yankee rule.

Then Brick Field jumped his mount forward and it crashed into Gilbert with a whinny, sending the raw-boned man floundering in the dirt. The redhead spurred after him as he tried to stagger upright, knocking him down again. Field was grinning coldly as he pranced his mount around Dal Gilbert as the man frantically tried to get out of the way. The sergeant was yanking back on the reins, lifting the horse on to its hind legs, when Hardy launched himself at the man, hit him with his shoulder and carried him out of the saddle.

They grunted as they hit the street, rolled, still locked together, and Field bared more teeth as he brought up a knee into Hardy's midriff, jerked an elbow at his eye. It took him just below the socket on the cheekbone and Hardy rolled away, head snapping back.

The redhead was on his feet, waving back the few soldiers who were starting towards him. He wiped the back of a hand across his nostrils, ran in at Hardy who was getting up from all fours. His boot took the Johnny Reb in the side, sending him spinning, and Field jumped after him, stomping with his heavy army boots.

On his back, Hardy caught a boot as it descended towards his face, managed to hold it, and wrenched savagely. Field grunted as his ankle twisted and then his big body followed and he floundered face down. Hardy threw himself on to the man's back, pounded his face into the ground.

The redheaded sergeant was obviously a tough man — look how he had shot Hardy in the canyon while being dragged by a panicked horse — and likely he had been brawling his way through the army for years. He spat a broken tooth as blood flooded down across his mouth and chin from his nostrils, wrenched around and kicked Hardy off, rolling quickly towards him and butting him on the forehead.

Hardy's skin split but he bounced away and when he got to his feet, swaying, bright lights dancing in front of his eyes, Brick Field was waiting for him with cocked, gnarled fists. The sergeant stepped in, prodding, feeling him out, moving about like a dancer. Hardy turned slowly, parrying the probing punches without much effort, eyes narrowed and concentrating on the Yankee's face. Field grinned through the blood on his face, enjoying it, as he lunged in a feint and brought over a haymaker.

His face was something to see when he realized Hardy wasn't where he had expected him. The man was right up against the sergeant and a blow that travelled less than six inches slammed Field in the belly. He gagged and instinctively stepped back — thereby giving Hardy room for a more powerful blow. And it came: a looping, whistling punch that cracked against the side of Field's jaw and turned his head so sharply some in the crowd expected to hear the neck snap. The redhead staggered, fighting for balance, and Hardy was after him, fists blurring as he beat the man to his knees with a flurrying barrage of blows that made the sergeant's ribs creak and his head hum and roar with pain. He hung there, swaying on his knees, bloody-faced, but still stubbornly refusing to give up.

'Looks like I'll have to finish this, Brick,' Hardy said, breathing heavily. 'I'm too damn tired to fight all day.'

Field made a valiant attempt to lunge to his feet but Hardy took a long step forward and a left and a right smashed Field down to the street where he lay, not quite out to it, but bleeding and hurting, unable to do anything more.

Hardy stepped back, a mite shakily, sucked at his swollen knuckles. He weaved to where Dal Gilbert was sitting and offered his hand to the man.

Gilbert looked up with his sunken eyes, moved his gaze to Hardy's hand — then spat into the palm and jumped to his feet unaided.

'Don't touch me, you gutless bastard!' he snarled, and the townsfolk who had been watching — *cheered*.

3

Coward!

A rifle butt slammed Hardy between the shoulders and he staggered forward, fighting to keep balance. Gilbert tripped him and the one-armed man was roughly shoved aside by a red-faced soldier who hit Hardy again with the rifle, this time in the kidneys.

Hardy sprawled on his face and the soldier closed, kicked him in the side as boots pounded and two more armed soldiers came running up. The man with the First Class stripes shoved aside the one who had done the kicking and motioned for his companion to stand back. He glared at the trooper who had knocked Hardy down.

'Get Sergeant Field on to his feet and cleaned up!' the man snapped, turned his attention to Hardy as the Reb got up slowly, holding a hand against his ribs. 'You're who, mister . . . ?'

Hardy explained briefly and the man arched his eyebrows.

'Yeah, got word you might be along . . . You and the sarge don't hit it off so well.'

Hardy touched the adhesive patch above his right ear. 'He put his brand on me — he didn't need to ride down Dal Gilbert, though.'

'I can take care of myself, Hardy!' the one-armed man snapped as a soldier held on to his arm. 'I don't need no yaller-back helpin' me out.'

The private first class frowned at Hardy. 'What's this 'yaller-back'? You did all right agin the sarge and he's a mean one. I've never seen him put down before, let alone k-o'd.'

'We have to talk here?' Hardy asked.

'If I say so, yeah.'

Hardy shrugged. 'This is my home town. It was almost one-hundred per cent Confederate.'

The private, youngish but with old

eyes, smiled crookedly. 'You bein' the 'almost'?'

Hardy shrugged. 'I was up in Idaho, had no convictions one way or another when war broke out. Decided to stay put and wait it out.'

The private wasn't smiling now. 'You never fought at *all*?' When Hardy didn't reply, his touch of friendliness disappeared. 'So — you played hidey-go-seek instead of doin' your duty. *Now* I see where the 'yaller-back' comes in.'

Hardy rubbed his aching back and eased his throbbing shoulders as well as he could. Field had been dunked in the horsetrough and, spluttering, weaved his way across, wiping his face on a kerchief. His eyes were deadly as he looked at Hardy, then shifted his gaze to the private.

'All right, Mace. He's mine — I'll settle with him in my own way and in my own good time.' He looked at the crowd and the soldiers. 'Get about your business, all of you.'

The soldiers stirred themselves and

began jostling the townsfolk along. As Gilbert started to join them, Field stopped him. 'Not you. No broken-winged damn Reb is gonna call me or my men *scum*.'

'Why not? It fits!' snapped Gilbert and Hardy sighed, stepping in quickly.

'Dal, take it easy. I've heard about the trouble this town has caused and see what it's got you? Just look around. The place is a dungheap! Look at the buildings, they — '

He paused, noticing for the first time, the charred timbers of a long-burned building half-way along Main. Beyond, near some temporary-looking corrals that held a dozen or so horses, army mounts by the size of them, were more charred ruins.

Suddenly, a beaming smile broke across Dal Gilbert's ravaged face. 'Recognize 'em, Hardy? Might be a leetle-bit tough, I guess. Both them places were standin' when you quit this town. This here was the general store — now what was it called . . . ? Oh,

41

yeah — *Hardy's Emporium*, that was it. An' down there . . . well, that was the town livery. *Hardy's Stables and General Livery*, the sign used to say. Now, wonder what could've happened to them places?'

He laughed. Some folk lingering despite the cussing and shoving of the soldiers, laughed with Gilbert. Brick Field shot Hardy a look.

'Guess you ain't got as many friends in this dump as you thought, Hardy.'

'Guess not.'

'Then you ain't gonna be much help to the colonel.'

'Why not? I didn't expect flags and a big parade . . . They'll listen when I talk to 'em, even if they just come to pelt me with rotten vegetables. They might be poor and look whipped, but they got brains and some of 'em'll think on what I say and see that it's the only way things are gonna work.'

Field pursed his split lips. 'Well, they call you *yaller-back*, but you seem to have more guts than I gave you credit for . . . When you gonna call this meetin'?'

'Why not right now?'

Field seemed surprised, then spread his hands. 'Yeah, why not. You men, start roundin'-up the townsfolk an' — where you want 'em, Hardy?'

Hardy looked steadily at the redhead. 'Down where the livery used to be — plenty of space there.'

Brick Field laughed, shaking his head. 'Damn, but I never did see a man get up like you after bein' kicked so many times in the balls! I better watch it — I could even get to like you, Hardy.'

'Now that *would* worry the hell outa me!'

★   ★   ★

The crowd was surprisingly subdued while Hardy spoke. There was heckling but nothing to worry him and the odd missile whizzed in his direction where he stood on an upturned rainbutt, but

43

he was able to dodge or parry all of them.

Under the severe guidance of Sergeant Brick Field and his counterpart, Sergeant Taggart, the man in charge of the contingent of soldiers at Hardyville, the crowd settled down and heard Hardy out.

He put a simple argument to them: more than half the town's menfolk — and some young boys — were missing from the group, because they had been killed in the war.

'Dyin' while fightin' for what they believed in, yaller-back!' a voice called and others roared agreement.

'But *dying*,' Hardy emphasized. 'They'll never come back. They died well, I have no doubt, but now you have to come to terms with the fact that the South *lost*. Wait! I didn't say *beaten* I said *lost*! Worn down, without supplies or arms, Lee had no alternative but to sign the surrender at Appomattox. That's past, and it's a *fact*. Now it's time to make the best of the peace.'

'We ain't seen much of this goddamn peace you're talkin' about!' yelled someone.

'And you won't as long as you fight the Reconstruction. Look, it's harsh and unjust in many ways, but just think if the boot was on the other foot — how would we treat the Yankees if they'd lost?'

'Don't you include yourself in how we do or don't act, you damn coward!' called Dal Gilbert. 'Sittin' it out up there in Idaho with plenty food and no danger. You got no right to tell us what to do!'

The crowd agreed with that.

Hardy let them settle down. 'You're right — but I'm not *telling* you. All I'm doing is asking you to think about what you do. Think of the consequences if you kick over the traces. You fight Colonel O'Connor's orders and he's *got* to dish out punishment. I dunno whether he enjoys doing it or not and I don't care — all I'm saying is, give him a mite more co-operation and see how much better things are. If they don't measure up, get yourself a petition and send it to him in Springfield.'

'He'll use it to wipe his ass!'

'Then send another. *I'll* take 'em in personally if you want. Maybe that sort of thing's not the answer, but neither is fighting him at every turn. This town'll soon be nothing more than burnt sticks if it keeps on resisting.'

'The South don't knuckle under to no Yankee, no matter what!'

There was a roar of agreement, but way back where Hardy couldn't see who spoke, a voice called, 'I've lost crops and furniture and money, because we fought them Reconstruction taxes. I got a family . . . I can't lose nothin' else but our home and after that, there won't be nothin' left to fight for. Reckon we could mebbe talk some more about what Hardy's been sayin'. His word don't carry much weight in this town no more, but — well, I'm mighty weary and beat down an' I want to get up and start workin' to give my family some kinda future. Like Hardy said, what we been doin' ain't the way.'

'Another yaller-back!'

'You up in Idaho with Hardy, too, while the war was on?' sneered a drink-slurred voice.

There was a brief silence and another, quieter voice said, 'Why don't you shut your mouth, Ferris? That was Bernie Doyle talkin', you drunken fool! He won the Silver Star at Shiloh, for Chris'sakes!'

There was a murmuring in the crowd and Hardy smiled faintly and climbed down from the rain butt. Field frowned.

'Quittin' already?'

'The right time to quit — for now. Doyle's words'll carry a lot of weight, more than mine. I know him. Unassuming feller, 'bout five-feet nothing, looks like he'd have trouble lifting a rifle — but you heard what they said about Shiloh. These folk'll listen to someone like him. 'Specially if I'm not around to remind 'em of where he got the notion to show a little co-operation in the first place.'

Field scowled. 'Aah, it ain't that easy!'

'Hell, no. But it's a *start*, Field! That's more than I hoped for when I rode in here.'

The redhead remained silent for a spell, watching the animated townsfolk arguing amongst themselves. 'What you mean about you not bein' around . . . ?'

Hardy's face was sober. 'Time I went to see my own family — or what's left of it.'

'You ain't goin' alone!'

'Be my guest.'

'I'll be more'n that: you won't be able to wipe your nose without me bein' there to check the kerchief first.'

Hardy grinned. 'Sounds like it's gonna be real fun.'

'Don't bet on it!'

★   ★   ★

It wasn't very far out of town to the spread, but to Hardy, it somehow felt like the endless trail drive up from Texas all over again.

Then suddenly it was over. There was reality now.

The ranch looked dilapidated even from a distance.

Sergeant Brick Field, still occasionally dabbing at his bleeding mouth, lowered his kerchief and remarked, '*That's* what you wanted to come home to?'

'Looked better last time I saw it,' Hardy said a little grimly. 'Don't see any ranch hands about — if there's only Lee and the kid . . . '

'That's all, far as I know. This is my first time out here but I know they had a goin'-over early on when O'Connor figured he had to show everyone just how tough he could be.'

Hardy looked at him sharply. 'What d'you call a 'going-over'?'

Field shrugged. 'What's it matter now? It's been and gone. If they're still feisty, you talk 'em around. That's your job — don't matter whether they're family or not. An' just a reminder: I ain't yet made up my mind whether to bring charges agin you for beatin'-up on me.'

Hardy allowed himself a thin smile. 'And here I was thinking we were gonna be friends.'

The redhead snorted. '*Me*! Friends with a Johnny Reb? That'll be the day the sun don't rise . . . '

They rode the rest of the way in silence.

No one appeared on the porch with its sagging railing even when they rode in past the empty corrals and the barn with vertical planks missing, both doors long gone. The house had shingles missing from the roof and a couple of river stones had fallen out of the chimney. A torn curtain fluttered wearily at a broken window.

'Looks deserted,' opined the sergeant, hand on his gun butt.

Hardy didn't reply, stepped down a little stiffly from the big black and thumbed his hat back off his leather-brown face.

'Hello the house! Lee! Larry! It's Deke . . . '

No answer.

Field had dismounted by now and had his gun in his hand, walking off to the side but looking intently at the house: a good soldier, Hardy thought grudgingly, taking no chances. Not that there seemed to be anything to worry about here . . .

The thought had no sooner formed than there was a *zzzippping* sound and Field swore as he dived for the ground, his campaign hat transfixed by an arrow. He rolled in behind the water pump and put a shot through a window, glass tinkling.

'Hold it! Hold it!' yelled Hardy starting to run for the porch. 'It's me! Your brother Deke!'

'An' who's that Yankee son of a bitch with you? One of your pards?'

Hardy wasn't sure if he recognized the voice or not. Larry's voice hadn't quite broken when he had left, but this was a strong, young-sounding voice.

'He's here with me, Larry! No trouble! I'm coming in so don't get edgy.'

'You open that door and I'll put an arrer through your throat!'

'For Chris'sakes, calm down! What the hell's wrong with you? We're family, you and me.'

'Only family I got is Lee! We don't have no brothers left alive!'

That stopped Hardy in his tracks. Field took a chance and started slowly to his feet. 'Son, you put down that bow and arrer — I know, you've heard about the Thompson brothers in Florida, figured they'd get around the 'no-gun' law for returnin' Rebs — but it won't work! It's been changed to no *arms or weapons* and that lets out bows and arrers. You and a lot of others are findin' that out the hard way!'

Hardy had heard about the Thompson brothers in the Florida Everglades, not allowed firearms because they had fought for the Confederacy, but to protect themselves from the predatory wildlife and to put food on the table for their families, they had taken to using a bow and arrow — with deadly results. They hadn't used the weapons against the occupying Yankee forces, but there was always that fear that someone else would get the notion.

'C'mon, kid — I'm not lookin' for trouble, but I'll shoot back if you let loose with one more arrow, I swear.'

He swore all right as a shaft thudded, quivering, into the hardwood box around the base of the pump, and he dived for cover. Hardy ran forward, launched himself through the rickety door of the house and into the gloomy and musty-smelling interior. He knew which window Larry had to be at and he charged into the parlour, saw a blurred shape turning towards him, hearing the slight click of the taut bowstring as an arrow was nocked. Then he was crowding the figure back and Larry yelled and crashed to the floor. And as Hardy snatched at the bow he saw the pair of crutches leaning against the window sill — and the empty lower trouser leg on the boy.

Larry sobbed in frustration more than anger as his big brother tore the bow from him and tossed it out the window, yelling to Field to hold his fire, that there was no more danger.

Field came in quickly through the back door — and there was a struggling girl with him. He shook her by the arm he was holding and she swung a blow at his face. He got his head aside in time, thrust her, stumbling, into the room.

Her fair hair flew wild as she lunged for Larry who was sprawled on the floor, shouldering Hardy aside. 'Larry, are you all right?'

'I'm — fine! Except *he's* in the damn house and I swore he'd never set foot in here again!'

He, of course, was Deke Hardy, and the boy, narrow-faced like his brother and sister, glared wildly. Hardy was shocked at the look of the boy: pale, gaunt, something wild in his eyes that he'd never seen before.

Lee was still beautiful, if a man took the trouble to peer beneath the rather sharp, hungry-looking features, but her eyes were dulled, too, and there was a hard defiance Hardy didn't remember from before although she had always been strong-willed enough. Her clothes were patched but tolerably clean and there was little friendliness in the way she stared at her big brother now.

'I didn't think you'd ever dare show your face around here again!' she said quietly, an edge of quavering anger in her words. 'Not after the disgrace you brought upon this family.'

Hardy remained impassive, aware that Field was watching him closely. Watching *all three of them* closely, the Remington pistol still in his hand. Larry started to pull himself up by the window sill and Hardy automatically stepped forward to help him. He stopped abruptly at the look of pure hatred on the youth's face, heard the breath hissing between his teeth.

'Get away from me!'

Lee shouldered Hardy aside once more and helped Larry up, got him his crutches. It was his lower right leg that was missing and Hardy felt sick: young Larry had been a fine runner as he remembered, always winning the foot races held as part of the Fourth of July celebrations. He had even talked about going East one day and competing in the big St Louis games for a lot of prize money.

'Where'd it happen?' Deke asked tightly.

Larry glared silently, then said forcefully, his eyes growing moist despite himself, 'Gettysburg! While you were lyin' back somewheres up in Idaho stuffin' yourself with grub and booze, *I* was lyin' in a water-filled ditch at the bottom of Little Big Top, tryin' to knot my belt around my leg to keep from bleedin' to death!'

'Happened to a lot of men, son,' Field said not unkindly, but Hardy, surprisingly, spoke sharply,

'Self-pity won't bring the leg back, Larry.'

He reeled as Lee's hand smashed him across the face.

'How dare *you* say a thing like that to — to your kid brother! He was in uniform, fighting, three days after his fourteenth birthday! While you — '

'While I was doing — whatever I was doing,' cut in Hardy harshly. 'Look, you don't know a thing about what I was doing during the war. You've listened to all the rumours and while I'm not denying there's some truth in some of them, a hell of a lot of them are way off the truth.'

'Whatever that may be!' she spat.

'Reckon you're fightin' a losin' battle, Reb,' the Yankee sergeant opined with something of a smirk.

'You stay the hell out of this!' Hardy snapped. 'Why don't you leave us alone while I try to talk some sense into these two.'

Field merely shook his head, glancing at Larry. 'That bow looked pretty good, kid, but don't make another.' He stepped forward, picked up the three arrows lying on the floor and snapped them under his boot.

'What are we supposed to use to protect ourselves?' demanded Lee, eyes blazing. 'There're cougars around here, the occasional bear — and *always* a species of rat or skunk that wears a blue uniform skulking about!'

Hardy frowned. 'You've had trouble?'

She laughed harshly. 'Oh, no, not really — just a little rape now and again, the odd plunder and pillage, a beating for Larry, theft of whatever livestock and food we might have managed to get together . . . '

Hardy's fists were knotted down at his sides as he set bleak eyes on the redhead. 'I wasn't told anything about that!'

Field shrugged. 'The men've been dealt with. It's over.'

The sound of Lee's bitter laughter brought goose-bumps to the back of Hardy's neck. He tried to reach for her arm but she stepped back swiftly, raising a hand, and Larry balanced precariously as he swung up one crutch and prodded Hardy in the midriff.

'You leave her alone! Leave us both alone! Get out of this house! It don't belong to you no more!'

Sergeant Field spoke quietly, 'I think that might be good advice, Hardy, you ain't gonna get any co-operation out of these two, not this day.'

'Not *any* day!' snapped Larry.

Hardy sighed. 'You could be right, Brick — I sure feel like a stranger here.'

'That's because you are,' Lee told him and maybe there was a hint of regret in her tone although she kept her half-starved face tight and angry. 'You'll never be anything to us, Deke. We don't know you and we don't want to know you — or anything about you. I guess you can remember where the door is . . . '

She stepped alongside Larry and together they left the room, the girl with her head held stiffly, unwavering gaze straight ahead, the boy lurching a little on his rough crutches.

As they rode slowly away, the redhead said, 'Sorry it had to be that way, Reb. I can see how it affected you.'

Hardy was surprised to realize Field meant it.

4

Armed and Dangerous

Colonel O'Connor leaned back in his chair and stretched out an arm to pick up a pencil. He turned this end-for-end on the desk edge as he looked at the seated Brick Field opposite.

'You're going soft, Sergeant.'

The redhead stiffened. 'No, sir!'

'You are — why didn't you bring the kid in? He'd violated Reconstruction Law.'

'I broke his arrows and tossed the bow into the river miles from the spread. I . . . figured they'd had a pretty rough time and — well, it seemed to me I'd get better co-operation from Hardy if I let things be.'

O'Connor pursed his heavy lips, nodded slowly. 'All right, that could be — and did you?'

'We rode to seven ranches durin' the four days we been away, Colonel. He ain't popular, but even the ones who took a pitchfork to him, listened. None of 'em said they'd co-operate, but you could see they was thinkin' about it.'

'You made promises in my name as instructed?'

'Yessir — I told 'em if they co-operate, it'll be better all round, no one has to starve, and they'd be dealt with fairly if there were any disputes. The usual stuff.'

'Not what you'd call a success, though, is it?'

Field looked uncertain. 'I reckon he might've got across to the townsfolk — through that medal winner, Bernie Doyle. Someone's gonna listen to him.'

'And I suppose Hardy learned about the . . . incidents at his sister's place?'

'She told him. Not in detail, but you could see him gettin' riled.'

O'Connor frowned. 'Yes. He's formidable when roused, is Deke Hardy. I witnessed his outraged fury when we rode on punitive expeditions among the Indians up north. Did he ask you for details?'

Details! Yeah, he asked. They hadn't ridden far from the ranch when Hardy had set those damn cold eyes on Field and said quietly, 'What happened to the men who raped Lee?'

Field was going to shrug it off, but instead looked straight at the Reb riding beside him and told him, 'One was shot, one jumped through a handy open window and bled to death in the street. The other was hanged . . . '

'Three of them — that was all?'

Field nodded. 'Drunk on some damn poisonous snakejuice some of your rebel friends had sold 'em. Out of their heads completely. Wore floursack masks and gloves, and long coats over their uniforms . . . '

'They weren't all that drunk then — not if they could think to do them things. They knew what they were about, seems to me.'

'Don't matter now — we caught 'em

and they're dead.'

'They pick out Lee's place special, or go to other spreads, too?'

'The hell's it matter now!' exploded Field. But Hardy's steady gaze never wavered and finally the redhead admitted, 'Yeah, they went on a bit of a rampage. Now leave it, damnit, Hardy! We got enough of a problem right now without botherin' about somethin' that happened a year ago.'

Then he returned to the present, nodding.

'Yeah, he asked, Colonel, and I gave him just the bare bones.'

'And where is he now?'

'I put him in that wooden lock-up shed we keep for soberin'-up the drunks. Hanrahan is on guard.'

O'Connor nodded. 'Good — but don't treat him too harshly. Not yet. We can still use him. In fact I *need* him for a spell yet. Headquarters are riding me to produce results in this area' — he leaned forward abruptly — 'and that's exactly what I intend to do! I clean up this neck of the woods and I'm on the way up . . . the *only* way to go, far as I'm concerned.'

The pencil snapped suddenly and Kyle O'Connor stared at it in surprise.

Sergeant Brick Field kept his face blank.

★   ★   ★

Deke Hardy stretched out on the narrow bunk in the small cell: Field could tell him it was a 'sobering-up' shed, but it was a jail cell as far as Hardy was concerned.

That was OK. He could savvy how they didn't want to let him run around free right now.

But that didn't mean he aimed to stay locked up.

Some of those ranchers, even while cussing him out for being a 'traitor' and a 'yeller-bellied coward' still managed to get across the kind of rough life they'd been leading under Colonel Kyle O'Connor's Reconstruction . . .

The Yankee had told the Missourians that they had to be prepared to make 'sacrifices' in order to bring the Reconstruction plan to fruition — telling this to people who had already sacrificed everything: the lives of their families, their stock and crops, any hoarded food and certainly what little money might have been set aside.

But O'Connor didn't just *tell* them, he *made them do it*! Made them sacrifice what pitiful assets they still had in the name of the great god Reconstruction. People were beaten, some crippled, others killed, still others brought to 'trial' where they faced long sentences on the chain gangs. The womenfolk were submitted to all kinds of indignities, no matter what their ages, from ten-year-old girls, to wrinkled grandmothers: O'Connor turned his men loose.

Of course, he claimed that when he heard of their behaviour he did what he could to bring them to heel. Harsh discipline for a few, the ultimate penalty for a very few others. No doubt he considered it a good thing, demonstrating his 'impartiality' but in reality many more crimes went unpunished than were brought to the Yankee-run court.

Hardy had known all along that he was going to be used. He knew O'Connor of old, knew the man had always been ambitious, had been prepared to do just about anything to gain promotion or simply to get his own way. He had seen it demonstrated over and over again while he had been scouting for the army.

Hardy had gone along with O'Connor so he could get the lie of the land and see just what was happening here. He had had to put things together himself, and it hadn't really surprised him to learn how bad they were. He had seen the Reconstruction at work in Texas, although it was claimed that Texas had been singled out for especially harsh treatment by the Yankees — no one was sure why, but it seemed that way.

Now he was pretty sure it was mighty rough going for *any* state or territory that had fought on the side of the Confederacy. Of course, it would have been the same in the northern states if the South had been victorious, but that didn't make any of this the more palatable.

He must have been crazy to think he could just drive those steers in and start up the ranch again.

OK, he'd found out the hard way he had been wrong and now he had to make other plans.

And they didn't include staying locked-up.

He went to the barred window in the heavy wooden door and rattled it. He saw the shadowy figure of the guard leaning against a corner of the hut, stealing a smoke, the cigarette cupped in his hand, the red glow briefly lighting part of his face as he drew in.

'Hey, guard! This slop bucket in here's overflowing and I need to go.'

'Use the floor.'

'Like hell. That may be the way you do it where you come from, but my pappy taught me right early that no animal with even half a brain fouls its own nest.'

The guard, Hanrahan, stirred, and came down to scowl at the dim shape of Hardy at the barred window.

'I ain't just sure exactly what you're sayin', Reb, but — don't — say — it — again!'

Hardy was ready when the rifle butt came up and tried to mash his fingers where they gripped the bars. He got his hand out of the way and Hanrahan swore, stumbled. Then Hardy's hands darted between the bars, fingers locking on the man's protruding ears, as he smashed him face-first into the door.

The guard moaned and the rifle fell with a clatter. He was dazed, but far from knocked out. He swore as he started to push back, hand fumbling at his belt. Hardy didn't release his grip, yanked viciously, again and again. Blood spattered his wrists and a little even touched his face. He shifted his grip to the man's tunic as Hanrahan's legs began to fold under him.

Grunting a little with the effort, Hardy managed to turn the man around, locked an arm about his neck, then stood on tiptoes as he reached out and down as far as he could for the belt. He felt the keys, yanked them free and pushed the unconscious man away from the door. He upended the near-empty slop-bucket, stood on it as he reached awkwardly, stretching through the barred window, and worked the key into the padlock. His arms were aching, his fingers numbed and fumbling before he got it snapped open. Hanrahan gave a couple of moans and stirred slightly.

This only spurred Hardy on as he strained to work the rusted iron bolt through its metal supports. It resisted when the strain of his body pressing against the door came on to the last inch or so. It took him precious minutes to figure out what was wrong.

Hanrahan was starting to sit up groggily now.

Hardy eased his weight off the door, just managed to free the bolt and kicked the door open violently as Hanrahan staggered upright. Actually he was only half-upright when the door smashed into him and knocked him back several feet into the dark yard behind the army barracks.

Hardy lunged out, kicked the dazed man in the jaw and Hanrahan once again went to sleep. The prisoner swiftly removed the gunbelt and its pouches of spare balls and paper cartridges, buckled it about his own waist. The pistol dragged at his left side, set for cross-draw as was usual for the army. Hardy spun, searched for the fallen rifle and snatched it up from against the wall, then dragged Hanrahan into the shed. He used the man's own trouser belt to tie his hands behind him, a blanket to bind his ankles and to blindfold and gag him on the bunk.

Then he locked the door again, and

71

started out into the darkness, realizing now that the gun he held was a Spencer carbine. He would like to have a Blakeslee cartridge box that held several pre-loaded tin magazines for sliding into the tube in the butt for fast reloading. But he couldn't have everything, he figured, and went in search of a mount. There were several horses for officers in a small corral over to the left and he made his way there, seeing with satisfaction the line of saddles thrown carelessly across the top rail, the pile of saddle-bags on the ground beneath.

He smiled as he looked around warily: could be his luck was changing for the better. Beside the saddle-bags he saw another pile and he figured some luckless dog-face would get his ass hauled for leaving Blakeslee cartridge boxes out in the open.

If they contained the usual six to thirteen tubes of ammunition for the Spencer as he hoped, he would be ready to take on the whole damn Reconstruction and anything O'Connor wanted to throw at him ... he was armed now and more dangerous than ever.

*   *   *

Hardy knew they would come looking for him out at the ranch but he had to go there, get things straightened away with Lee and young Larry. He still felt a cold knot form in his belly when he thought about his kid brother and his missing leg.

Of all the lousy things ... Long ago he had given up cussing things that couldn't be changed, but it sure was a rough deal for the kid.

He was forking a sturdy sorrel as he came in over the ridge, the half-moon rising over the distant hills now and flooding the flats with a pale light. There were no lights in the ranch house, but he had expected that.

He dismounted and led the horse in. There were four Blakeslee cartridge boxes hanging from the saddle-horn, two each side, and each box held thirteen tubes of seven-cartridges for the Spencer. He was just about ready to start a war!

The pistol was a Remington — Beals in .44 calibre, and had to be loaded chamber-by-chamber, but there was a pouch stuffed with sixty ready-measured tubes of powder. He would only have to slip one into each chamber, ram the ball on top, thumb the percussion caps on to the nipples and he was ready for bear . . .

'Just where the hell you figure you're goin', mister?'

Hardy almost jumped out of his skin as the voice came to him out of the pitch darkness of the doorless barn as he led the horse inside. *Damn!* They must have left a man here to watch the ranch.

A gun hammer ratcheted back to full cock.

'You ain't answered me yet, mister!'

Hardy froze. 'Now I don't believe in ghosts, but damned if you don't sound like old Flapjack . . . '

'What's this 'old', feller? Hey, Deke — that you?'

They both stepped into the pale light washing through the doorway at the same time, grinned, gripped hands, Flapjack holding his gun down at his side now.

'They told me all you fellers had been killed in the stampede — or shot afterwards.'

'Yeah, well that's what happened to the rest,' Flapjack said quietly. 'I got shot in the back and in all the dust my hoss ran back out of the canyon and we managed to get into a draw and I stayed there till the Yankees left with the dead and what cows they'd managed to round up. Was feelin' mighty poorly by that time, but I backtracked into them hills we'd crossed before reaching the canyon, holed up in a cave. Must've gone into fever for a few days, but it broke and I was able to do a little doctorin', made my way down here when I was feelin' better . . . Lee and

Larry nursed me through the last bit and I figured I'd pay 'em back by keepin' watch out here.' His voice hardened. 'Seein' as what had happened before.'

'I don't have the details of that yet,' Hardy said, and they made their way to the house and Hardy felt strangely nervous about meeting his sister and kid brother once again.

They had been sleeping lightly and were awake when the two men entered. Hardy stopped in the kitchen as Larry stoked the fire, and he noticed how well the kid managed with the crutches. Lee stared at him and he faced her, nodded tentatively, waiting to see what she would do.

He was unprepared when she let out a small cry and ran at him, and threw her arms about him, crushing herself against him. *What the* . . . But he naturally slid his arms about her.

'Oh, Deke, Deke! Can you ever forgive me for what I thought — what I *said* to you! I-I didn't know! Flapjack told us and . . . '

Hardy's gaze met the old cowboy's and Flapjack merely shrugged, spreading his hands. 'Figured it was time someone set the record straight.'

Larry Hardy came across, rested his crutches under his arms and thrust out his right hand, looking awkward. 'I owe you an apology, too, I guess, big brother . . . '

Hardy gripped firmly with the bony hand and grinned. 'Forget it. With all those stories going around — '

'We should've known better than to listen to them,' cut in Lee. 'Now sit you down. We've managed to salt away a little coffee and even some bacon.'

'I'd best not stay long,' Hardy said and told them of his escape from Springfield. 'They might not find Hanrahan for a while, but this is the first place they'll look for me when they do.'

Larry dropped into a chair while Flapjack went outside again to keep watch. The kid had a look of admiration in his eyes now. 'Did you really blow up seven Yankee supply trains?'

Hardy smiled faintly. 'Eight. Well, strictly speaking, I didn't blow it up: it derailed on a bridge where I'd loosened a rail, dropped into the river. It was carrying powder and ammunition and went up with a helluva bang . . . '

'And you worked undercover for the Confederacy all those years and no one ever knew!' Lee said, fussing at the stove with the coffee pot. 'Everyone around here treated us like lepers when word came down that you were sitting out the war in Idaho, refusing to fight for either side.'

'We deliberately spread those stories, so I could move around more freely — and no one, including the Yankees, took much notice of what I was doing or where I went.'

'Did you get a medal?' asked Larry eagerly.

'Medals don't mean much, Larry.'

'But did you get one?'

'They said there was one waiting for

me, but I never went and got it. Look, what're you going to do? Flapjack will have told you about the cows I was trying to bring up . . . you're having it pretty damn rough and it's not going to get better very soon. We'd best make other plans.'

'We can put up with whatever they throw our way now we know you ain't the yaller-back folk've been sayin',' said Larry and Hardy swiftly held up a finger.

'You keep that to yourself, Larry. If O'Connor finds out that I did all that sabotage, he'll have me shot.'

Lee brought coffee: it was weak but hot. 'The thing is, Deke, what're *you* going to do? You're on the run now and O'Connor won't show you any mercy after your escape.'

'Flapjack says he knows about some ex-Rebs living up in the hills down in the Indian Territory.'

'That's *outlaw* territory!' Larry said.

'What I did up in Idaho made me an outlaw years ago. It won't be any different for me living in the Territory.'

'But what will you do?' Lee insisted.

'Not sure, but I can make sure someone keeps an eye on you and Larry. Now, I can't stay for long. If they find me here you'll suffer right alongside me.'

She put a hand on his shoulder as he made to rise, her eyes gleaming. 'Oh, not yet, Deke! Please don't go yet! We haven't seen you for so long . . . '

Against his better judgement, Hardy allowed his sister and brother to persuade him to stay a while longer.

They confirmed that their father had died as O'Connor had described. Their other two brothers, Luke and Kelvin, had died fighting for the Confederacy, both killed on the same day at Gettysburg . . . three days after Larry had lost his leg to a Yankee cannon ball.

'So we're the only Hardys left in this neck of the woods,' Lee said.

'What happened to Cousin Joe and Uncle Tate?'

'You must've seen the burned-out

remains of the store and livery in town,' Lee said, tight-lipped. 'O'Connor was told they had set the fires themselves so as to frustrate his men. So, Joe and Uncle Tate were taken away and we heard later they had been shipped north to some prison camp. No one's heard anything about them since.'

Hardy looked grim. 'That damn town's got plenty to answer for!'

'Yeah!' agreed Larry readily. 'Lee an' me would've starved if we hadn't took care of ourselves. None of the townsfolk gave us any help . . . '

'Well, maybe we'll — '

None of them realized just how much time had passed and later it transpired that old Flapjack had fallen asleep in the barn: he was still recovering from his wound and fatigue had over-whelmed him.

Which was why he never saw nor heard the Yankee patrol arriving as they surrounded the ranch.

5

No Escape

The first the people in the ranch house knew of the arrival of the Union posse was when a bullet smashed in the remaining glass of the kitchen window.

Lee gasped as Hardy moved like an arrow, straight for the lamp, sweeping it off the table and into the fireplace where it smashed, flared briefly and then the kitchen was plunged into darkness.

'Down on the floor!' Hardy snapped, the Spencer in his hands now as he duck-waddled across to the broken window.

'What is it?' asked the girl shakily.

Hardy didn't reply. He heard Larry's crutches clatter as the youth got down on the floor awkwardly.

'Better give up, Hardy!' called Sergeant Brick Field. 'You timed it wrong — Hanrahan was due to be relieved an hour after you broke out. You're surrounded now. Come out.'

Lee heard Hardy swear softly. 'The hell's happened to Flapjack?' he said aloud.

'Gimme a gun, Deke!' Larry said, dragging himself across the floor. 'I can shoot pretty good.'

'No, Larry — you'll be in enough trouble just because I'm here in the house. You start shooting back and they'll hang you.'

'They got to get me first!'

'Quit talking like that! You just keep your head down — and see that Lee does the same.'

Two more guns crashed from the direction of the barn.

'Damn! Looks like they've found Flapjack!'

'Deke!' Brick Field called. 'We've got the old man! You better throw down your guns and walk out!'

Hardy, watching with his eyes just above the window sill, saw two dark shapes making for the corner of the house. Automatically, he brought up the Spencer, levered a shell into the breech, manually cocked the hammer and got off his shot. An instant later he fired a second time. A man cried out in the night and he saw one shadow drop, writhing, clawing at his leg. The other man, on all fours, grabbed the wounded soldier and dragged him back into the shadow of the barn by his collar.

There was a crash of gunfire and bullets tore at the ranch house, splinters flying, glass shattering, lead buzzing from the stone fireplace. Lee crouched under the table, arms over her head. Larry lay beside her, one arm across her shoulders.

There was shouting out there and the firing dwindled, finally stopped. Field called again.

'You can see you're out-numbered, Deke. We can shoot the place to matchwood. *And* we've got the oldster.

He wounded one of my men and that's a hangin' matter, you know. You're between a rock and a hard place, feller.'

'Shoot him, Deke!' hissed Larry. 'He's down by the front corner of the barn — I can tell by his voice. Shoot into the shadows and you'll nail the son of a bitch!'

Hardy sighed. 'That'd only get us all killed.'

'So? Better'n knucklin' under to them damn Yankees!'

'Larry, the war's over. You can resist but you don't have to die ... ' He raised his voice suddenly. 'If I come out, what about Lee and Larry?'

'Judas, Deke, you ain't gonna *deal* with 'em!'

'Shut up a minute, kid!'

'Deke, you can't trust them!' Lee said quietly, her voice a tremble.

'Don't see that I have much choice ... can't let 'em swing Flapjack.'

After a short silence, Field called, 'I got the word of the colonel, Deke, that your kinfolk won't be touched.'

Hardy was silent a moment. 'O'Connor's there with you?'

'Sure.'

'Then I want his word that Lee and Larry and Flapjack won't be harmed.'

'You just got it, damn you!' Field sounded annoyed.

'I want to hear the colonel say so!'

'The colonel don't do any shoutin' these days! You got his word through me.'

'Give me a gun, Deke! Please!' Larry started crawling towards Hardy but stopped when his big brother snapped at him.

'Stay put, damnit! Look, if O'Connor's out there I can deal with him. He won't lower himself by shouting across the yard so I'm going to have to go out. You two stay put — damnit, Larry, I said *stay put!*' He turned to the window. 'I'm coming out, Brick — just me. Don't send any men in. I want to talk with the colonel.'

A pause. Then, 'OK. The colonel agrees. But you toss your guns out first through the window. Rifle *an'* six-gun.'

Reluctantly Hardy obeyed and as he stood and made for the door, Larry said, 'I'm beginnin' to wonder about them stories of your sabotagin' the Yankees after all, Deke!'

'Larry!' snapped Lee. 'That's not fair! Deke's doing the best he can. But, Deke, I'm scared. I just don't trust *any* of them.'

'Can't see any other way, Lee . . . '

Hardy wrenched open the door and stepped out into the night, hands raised. Moonlight glinted dully from the rifle barrels as soldiers stepped forward, covering him. He saw Brick Field and Colonel O'Connor outside the barn.

There was a figure stretched out on the ground, and Hardy recognized Flapjack, paused briefly, then ran towards the man. A soldier stepped into his path, menacing him with his rifle. Hardy knocked the weapon aside, punched the man in the face and as he lunged for the supine Flapjack, he heard gun hammers cocking.

'Let him be!' snapped O'Connor quietly, as Hardy dropped to one knee beside the old man.

He put his hands under Flapjack's shoulders and felt the wetness of fresh blood there as he half-lifted the old cowboy. Flapjack groaned, opening his eyes.

'Take it easy, pard. The old back wound's opened up.'

The old man clawed at Hardy. 'Sorry, Deke . . . fell . . . asleep. Woke up with the barn . . . full . . . full of Yankees. Grabbed for my gun — still half-asleep — but they slugged me . . . '

Hardy turned his head, jaw like a rock, looking towards O'Connor. 'He needs a doctor.'

'Too late for that. He was a fool to go for his gun.'

'You heard him! He woke up with a fright! Just automatically reached for it! Do something, damn you!'

Colonel O'Connor looked coldly at Hardy. 'You let me down, Deke. Not only that, you've made me look a fool. I went easy on you and look how you've repaid me.'

'Never mind me. I'll take whatever you decide to hand out — just do something for Flapjack.'

'Well, with a name like that, I suppose we could attempt to flip him, eh?' O'Connor giggled and some of the soldiers laughed outright.

Brick Field wasn't one of them.

Hardy eased Flapjack down and suddenly he was moving with the speed of a striking snake, coming up and smashing his fist under Kyle O'Connor's jaw. The colonel grunted as he was slammed back into the line of soldiers, dragging three of them down with him.

Hardy made to move in, his rage getting the better of him, but Brick Field stepped in almost casually and gunwhipped him to his knees. He stood beside the Reb, twisting his fingers in the man's shirt and keeping him from falling all the way.

'You're a goddamned fool, Hardy!'

Deke, semi-conscious, started to struggle, but Field thrust him forward so that he fell to the ground and a soldier placed a boot between his shoulders, pressing his rifle muzzle into the back of Hardy's throbbing head.

Field helped the colonel up and the big man shrugged him off angrily. He stepped forward and kicked Hardy solidly in the ribs.

'Tie him up!'

As soldiers moved to obey, the sergeant asked, 'What about the oldster, Colonel?'

O'Connor looked down at the unconscious Flapjack, rubbing at his throbbing jaw. Then to Field's surprise, the man smiled slowly.

'Get him back to town for medical attention — I want him to get the best, understand? I want the son of a bitch to *live*!'

No, Field *didn't* understand — yet it didn't surprise him unduly, for he knew the colonel had a devious, evil mind, and if he wanted Flapjack alive, then he knew it wasn't going to be a pleasant experience for the oldster.

As he gave orders there was a yell from some of the soldiers out in the the yard.

'Fire! Fire!'

Colonel Kyle O'Connor wasn't a man much given to swearing. 'My hat!' was about the closest he came, although when truly upset — as just now after Hardy's attack — he had been known to cut loose with the occasional expletive. Now, when he saw the flames bursting from the ranch house, he swore savagely and briefly.

Spluttering, he screamed at the soldiers in his fury. 'Put it out! Put it out, you goddamned fools! Oh, Jesus Christ almighty! Why have I been cursed with this Hardy family! What in *hell* have I done to deserve these *bastards* blighting my life. *Get that fire out, I said!*'

The men ran for the pump but it had never worked well for years and now only a trickle came out despite the men working the handle frantically.

At the house, Lee Hardy staggered out on to the porch, slipped and fell through the broken railing. Brick Field ran forward and grabbed her by the arm and he hauled her to her feet, shaking her.

'The hell're you playing at, you little fool!' he hissed.

She clawed at him. 'Larry! Get Larry out! He's gone crazy, said he won't let you Yankees take our home . . . you've taken everything else but you won't get the house!'

Field looked at the flames licking at the old timbers, squinted against the wall of heat. 'If your brother's still in there . . . '

'He *is*, damn you! Do something — *please!*'

He pushed her into the arms of a couple of soldiers and leapt up on to the burning porch. He couldn't get in the door, jumped down, ran around to the rear but it was just as bad. He found one of Larry's crutches under the window, likely where the kid had thrown it before attempting to climb out . . .

'Larry!' the redhead roared. 'Grab a blanket and try to get out the door! Do it now or it'll be too late.'

It was already too late.

Inside, Larry lay unconscious on the parlour floor, his second crutch burning a couple of feet from his outstretched fingers. When he had been unable to get out of the kitchen window, he had tried to get back to the front entrance but by then the smoke had become an impenetrable fog and he had cannoned into the door frame, knocking himself semi-conscious. He fell, lost his crutch, tried to drag himself forward, but the thick, roiling smoke choked him and he collapsed with too little oxygen reaching his brain . . .

Moments later, the roof caved in, dumping a ton of blazing timbers over his body.

*   *   *

They had manacles on Deke Hardy now as he stood before O'Connor's desk in the Springfield office. The colonel's jaw was swollen and bruised and there was no trace whatsoever of friendliness in his cold eyes as he stared at the rebel.

'You let me down, Deke. You and your blasted family!' He stood and walked restlessly around his desk. The two soldiers guarding Hardy slid their eyes sideways, obviously mighty leery of their commander's mood. O'Connor stopped in front of Hardy. 'We could have had a good relationship, mutually beneficial, but you chose to defy me.'

'You were using me. There were too many claims about how your men had robbed and beaten the people around here. Folk were becoming too defiant. You just wanted me to make things easier for you . . . I changed my mind, that's all.'

'Well, I'll handle that later. Right

now, I'll bring you up to date on what's happened. Thanks to your stupid breakout and going back to your ranch, you apparently inspired your kid brother to resist us and in doing so he lost his life . . . '

'I'm laying the blame for that at your feet, Kyle,' Hardy told him coldly.

O'Connor seemed unmoved. 'Your friend Flapjack is recovering from his bullet wound. His age may go against him, but we'll do our best to keep him alive.'

Hardy frowned. 'That sounds just a bit *too* humane for you.'

The colonel smiled. 'Yes, I suppose it does. But I want Flapjack alive so he can stand trial — and be sentenced. Just as you will be.'

'To hang?'

'Oh, my hat, *no*! Deke, you never did understand my approach to punishing Indians and renegades when we were up north . . . but you should remember I had a reputation for being ruthless, implacable . . . and mighty vengeful.'

He seemed proud of it.

Proud of all the brutality and slaughter.

Hardy remembered, all right, and right now wished he didn't.

'So, you and Flapjack, will not hang. I have decided you have done the cause just too much harm and it's only fitting that you make reparation.'

'You know neither of us has a red cent, thanks to you.'

'Ah, yes — but you have muscles! Years of work left in you. There are special camps where such offenders as you and your friend can be sent. One is called High Heaven — a joke, of course, but you may've heard of it.'

'A slave camp! I thought your Congress abolished those long ago . . . '

'Well, officially, yes, but I managed to keep one going — and you and your friend are going there.'

Hardy felt a chill knot his belly. 'And Lee . . . ?'

'Lee? Oh, yes, your sister. Cleaned up rather well, I'm told. Well, of course, she'll have to do her bit, too, to repay her debt to the Union. So I will put her where she can do exactly that: in a place known as one of our 'comfort' houses for the use of our soldiers . . . you understand what I mean, Deke? Oh, stop it, man, stop it! You can't reach me and those manacles can be tightened even more, you know! Take him away and start him on his way to the camp. I don't want to set eyes on him again. One last thing, Deke. There can be no escape. That camp has an unblemished record. Every escape attempt has ended fatally — for the fools who tried it. But if *you* wish to try just the same . . . ' He spread his hands and smiled coldly. 'Be my guest!'

6

Heaven and Hell

The closest to heaven that the High Heaven 'Rehabilitation' Camp came was its elevation — 5,000 feet up on the south face of the Cherokee Breaks.

From the rear of the enclosed, near-airless prison transfer wagon, Deke Hardy could just manage to see part of the range through a gap in the heavy iron-wood boards. There was a dusting of snow on the highest peaks but the slopes where the camp was situated were free of the glistening white powder. Much timber had been cleared and he could even make out the black maw of the tunnel the prisoners were driving through the mountain, down at about the 2,000 foot level.

At present this was to be part of the new Transcontinental Railroad the

Union was so frantically building as part of the reconstruction of the country. Later it would be considered to be too far south and the whole project would be abandoned. Meanwhile, 'non-conformist' ex-Confederate prisoners were being used as slave labour. Loss of life was horrendous, as water from melting snow seeped through constantly, weakening the roof despite bracing. There had been several cave-ins but they were laboriously cleared and the work continued. If a man died, there was no problem in finding a replacement . . .

Hardy was with four other 'non-conformist' prisoners crammed into the small, heavy box drawn by a team of four horses. A driver and armed guard sat on the high, narrow seat. Four armed soldiers rode with the wagon, two in front, two behind, all of them cursing this escort duty that was not only tedious but mighty gruelling once they hit the mountain trail.

The journey from Springfield had

lasted two days so far and the men had eaten only once during that time and been given water twice. The air was thick with the stench of sweat and human waste for there were no relief stops unless the guard or driver needed them. The prisoners remained cramped and hungry in the gloomy wooden box.

It was now the afternoon of the third day. Tomorrow morning they would arrive at the camp and they speculated on what kind of pig slop they would be fed at High Heaven — or if they would be fed anything at all.

There was little conversation and when there was Hardy was not included in it. He was considered an outcast, a man these ex-Confederate soldiers regarded as a coward who had sat out the war in comfort and safety in Idaho, a land of plenty. Hardy knew this but he was damned if he was going to even try to convince them otherwise. They were men who had returned to their homes, battle-weary, half-alive, looking to make a new start, rebuild their lives.

Like others who had come under the authority of Colonel Kyle O'Connor they were soon disillusioned, stripped of their few remaining possessions in the name of *Reconstruction* — and any hopes they might have nurtured.

'You ask me,' ventured a bearded man named Bowker, 'they ought've called it *Destruction* — seems they're settin' out to tear down what's left of the South an' grind it into the ground.'

'It's bad in Kansas,' answered another man, 'an' my cousin in Texas says he's never goin' back down there after what he seen.'

'Lee should never've surrendered.'

'We'd all be dead if he hadn't!'

'We might be better off!' Bowker said bitterly. 'This is no more'n a livin' hell an' the place we're headed for is s'posed to be hell itself!'

'You listen to too many rumours,' Hardy said and through the half-light he felt their hostile gazes upon him.

'What would you know about it?' snapped Bowker.

'As much as you — which is next to nothing. We'll find out what it's really like when we get there, not before.'

'Nobody asked you!'

'No, stay out of it, Hardy! We don't want no planted goddamn spy buttin' in on our conversations!'

Hardy figured that was too stupid a remark to require an answer, but the others started verbally abusing him and he closed his ears to their profanity until suddenly their words were cut off — by the crash of gunfire.

One of the men in the driving seat grunted and Hardy heard the clatter and a moan as someone pitched off the wagon which lurched violently. Likely it was the driver, dropping the reins as he fell, he thought, pressing his face so hard against the warp between the planks that splinters tore at his bearded cheek: he hadn't shaved since arriving back in Missouri.

'*Attack!*' a distant voice yelled, one of the soldier escort. 'We're under attack!'

The sides of the wagon shuddered

under a series of ragged hammer-blows and Hardy figured they were just a few stray bullets rather than a volley directed at the vehicle. The wagon had ground to a halt now and Hardy distinctly heard the *thunk!* of a bullet striking flesh. A man half-moaned, half-screamed above, and his body must have struck the front wheel as he fell for the wagon jerked momentarily, rocking slightly.

'The hell's goin' on!' Bowker snarled, trying to pull Hardy away from the crack. Hardy elbowed him roughly in the midriff and he fell back gasping on top of his friends.

By God! he thought. This looks like a *rescue* attempt.

He glimpsed the soldiers scattering, awkwardly firing their Spencers. One man's horse went down and he was thrown heavily, quickly scrambled away across the slope to drop behind a boulder, abandoning his rifle, huddling into a ball, arms covering his head.

Next, Hardy saw a horseman clad

from shoulders to ankles in a dark-brown slicker and wearing a flour-sack hood with ragged eyeholes riding out from behind a boulder, rifle to his shoulder. Another of the escort toppled from the saddle, skidding several feet down the slope, unmoving after coming to rest.

The remaining two soldiers spurred away up the mountain trail, shooting wildly but only intent on getting away. Gunfire followed them, bullets spouting gravel behind them.

'Save your ammo!' a voice bawled, not the small man in the brown slicker that Hardy could see, but someone else out of his line of vision.

The other prisoners were yelling, jabbing at him, demanding to know what in hell was happening.

'Someone's rescuing us!' Hardy snapped, hardly believing it himself. 'Looks like at least three men, all dressed in slickers and hoods.'

'Watch out!' Bowker yelled suddenly. 'We're goin' over!'

The men had all tried to press against the same wall as Hardy, and the wagon had apparently stopped on a slope that gave it a slight lean. The extra weight all on one side toppled it with a violent jolt and a squealing and wild whickering of the team as the reins pulled two of them down. The wagon slid only a short distance before stopping and while the men tried to untangle themselves, a voice called. 'Get away from the door! We've gotta use black powder to blow the bolt!'

'You'll kill us!'

'Just stay away from the door — here we go!'

There was a heavy thud and the wagon shuddered and choking smoke billowed into the interior as the door buckled and fell partly open, one corner jamming against the ground. The prisoners rushed for the opening, chains rubbing and clanking and tangling. Someone outside grasped the door's edge and shouldered it open a few more inches. The men tumbled out one by one, blinking, fighting to regain their balance, ears ringing as they slid and stumbled on the loose scree.

A rider came alongside Hardy, quickly dismounted and unshackled him with a key. He tossed it to Bowker who immediately went to work on his own shackles. The rider turned to Hardy.

'Climb up. Them two troopers are high-tailin' it for the camp and they'll be back soon with help.'

There was a yell upslope and Hardy saw another of the hooded rescuers dragging the soldier who had hidden behind the boulder without attempting to fight. The man was struggling, sobbing, repeating over and over, *'Don't hurt me! I've got a family! I've fought at Gettysburg, The Wilderness and Vicksburg, and both Manassis, one and two! I just cain't fight no more! Please don't hurt me!'*

The one in the slicker and hood flung the cringing man to the ground and curled a lip as he drew back a boot.

'You yaller-bellied Yankee bastard!'

Hardy lunged forward and shoved the man back roughly so that he stumbled and sat down with a thud. He started to bring up his pistol but Hardy kicked it out of his hand.

'Leave him be,' he said quietly, gesturing to the distraught man. 'He's right. If he fought at all those places, he's had enough . . . no one can expect him to fight any more.'

'Judas, an' I just risked my neck to save you!' the slickered man said, getting up, but the short man who had freed Hardy came across.

'Hardy's right. No sense in abusin' this poor son of a bitch. Turn him loose and let's ride.'

'Yeah, I'll turn him loose, all right! Buck naked, so everyone can see the yeller streak down his backbone!'

So saying the hooded man started tearing off the Yankee's uniform and the man made no resistance: he had been destroyed by the war and perhaps had just been getting back some way to normal when the rescue attack had sent him over the edge. Hardy had seen men crack before, long after the battles that caused it had faded.

'Give me the clothes,' Hardy said as the naked man, oblivious to everything it seemed, climbed to his feet and started to run away towards the trees.

The man who had stripped him laughed, and Hardy snatched the clothes, pushed the man aside, growling, 'Leave the poor bastard be. Can't you see he's sick in the head?'

The masked man scoffed. Hardy mounted behind the short man, eager to get going. 'Where we headed?' he asked, holding the uniform awkwardly.

'A box canyon to the south,' the rescuer replied lifting his reins.

'A *box* canyon in any direction is bad news,' Hardy told him. 'One way in, same way out. I know a place, back towards Hardyville. On the far edge of the badlands, beyond the salt pans.'

The man in front half-hipped to look

at him from behind his mask. 'Ain't nothin' out there but dried-up water-courses.'

'One of them leads to a ravine where there's still good water — and there are *two* ways out.'

The rescuer hesitated, then lifted the reins, turning the horse in the direction Hardy had indicated calling to the others, 'Hardy's takin' us somewhere safe.'

'He better!' growled one man menacingly.

Two prisoners had caught up the horses of the soldiers who had lost them and the others had unharnessed mounts from the wagon team, allowing the others to run free. Dropped rifles had been collected, as well as the ammunition pouches and handguns from the guard and the dead soldier. The driver hadn't been armed.

'Where'd you get hold of guns?' Hardy asked the man in front of him as they rode away from the mountains.

'Stashed away. You'd be surprised at

how many guns O'Connor *ain't* found yet.'

Hardy smiled thinly. He was pretty sure he knew who this man was now: he figured it was Bernie Doyle.

★   ★   ★

When they reached the ravine, he found out he was right as soon as the man removed his slicker and hood.

'Not usually one to look a gift hoss in the mouth, Bernie, but just what the hell are you doing here?'

Doyle, barely a half-inch over five feet, ran a hand through his stringy hair which was dusted with a little residual flour from the sack he had used as a hood. Doyle was small but perfectly proportioned, like a half-grown man, or an over-grown boy. There was a scar on one cheek that Hardy didn't remember and later Doyle told him it was from a Yankee bayonet at Shiloh. He looked worried, but Hardy recalled that that was the normal look for Bernie Doyle:

110

he had *always* found something to worry over.

'O'Connor came down on us harder than ever. Figured your kickin' over the traces might give the rest of us ideas, I guess.' Doyle's voice hardened. 'They took my house and land, which was all I had left, kicked us out. Others had their places burned ... maybe it wasn't much, but we tried what you suggested, Deke: we tried to co-operate and look what it got us!'

'I guess I can shoulder the blame for that, all right,' Hardy said quietly. 'I knew O'Connor likely couldn't be trusted but I thought it was worth a chance: I'd seen him do some decent things when I knew him while I was scouting ... Figured we should all make the best of things because the country sure does need to get organized again.'

'No, you made sense to me, Deke. I'd had a bellyful of fightin' and truth is I was glad the war was over, didn't really care that the Union had won — just so long as there was some kinda peace. But we ain't gonna get that with O'Connor runnin' things.'

'Well, the Union authorities want the country to get on its feet again with a real peace. Men like O'Connor ain't gonna last for much longer. Someone's gonna realize he's doing more harm than good and the last thing they want is to stir up the South into another revolt.'

'Well, we're stuck with him for now. By the by, the wife was tryin' to earn a few cents by cleanin' up some of the Yankee places, includin' their comfort houses. She saw Lee and she told her you was a saboteur durin' the war, workin' undercover for the South all along . . .'

Hardy held his gaze, then nodded. 'Never have been one to take orders, Bernie, you know that. I'm better when I can be my own boss. Had a few fellers helping me, *Hardy's Rangers* we called ourselves.'

Bernie Doyle, having been joined by

the others now — men Hardy recognized — Dal Gilbert, Billy Dysart and Hondo McLane — wiped his right palm down his trousers and offered his small hand to Hardy. 'We all owe you an apology, Deke.'

'Accepted,' Hardy said, grinning and gripping with Doyle. The others shook his hand, too, even Dal Gilbert. 'Now I see why you all wore slickers — they'd have picked you out right away, Dal, with only one arm.'

Gilbert nodded, then gestured to the other prisoners standing back in a group. 'What about them?'

Hardy glanced at the filthy, ragged men who resembled scarecrows, realized he must look just the same. 'Well, I guess it's every man for himself — or we all join up and try to give O'Connor the worst headache he's ever had.'

Surprisingly, no one hesitated: they all agreed that that was the best thing to do; harass the hell out of O'Connor.

7

Phantom Enemy

The ravine was really a long, narrow valley, dropping suddenly below the level of the surrounding country, not unlike the Palo Duro on the Texas Panhandle. It was not as large and there were no buffalo, but there was game and plenty of water and graze.

'How come you know about this place?' Doyle asked Hardy.

'My grandpappy showed me when I was a kid. He used to come here sometimes and kind of . . . commune with nature. He had a little Cherokee in him, you know.'

'Well, it's dark now and I better be gettin' back to town . . . family's with the wife's sister, but the house is bustin' at the seams. We'll have to stay till we get someplace else.' Doyle was

114

returning so as to be able to keep in touch with the situation in town and also to make it look like he'd had nothing to do with the rescue of Hardy and the others. Dal Gilbert and Billy Dysart were going with him but Hondo McLane was staying behind with Hardy and the men who had been with him on the way to the prison camp.

Doyle scrubbed a hand over his stubbled face. 'I was kinda thinkin' . . . mebbe I could move the family out here, build a cabin — we could live here, I reckon. You have any objections, Deke?'

'It's not my place, Bernie, but I wouldn't do it just yet. O'Connor is going to tear up the countryside for a while. Anyone moving out will look suspicious to him. What I want to do is get Lee out of that damn whorehouse. And then I'll have to figure something for Flapjack . . . '

'I can get the general lay of the land, but I reckon O'Connor will be watchin' 'em both mighty closely. Specially Lee. He'll know you'll try to get her out.'

Hardy nodded. 'I'm working on it. But we need spare horses — '

'There's a mustang camp out at Bedloe Springs. Just a bunch of soldiers and a coupla civilian bronc busters. They're gettin' a string together for the army.'

Dal Gilbert supplied this information and Hondo McLane, a man who never said much as a rule, spoke up.

'We can git ourselves outfitted then. I know a way into Bedloe Springs that no one but the Injuns use.'

'Up over the ridge?' asked Hardy and when Hondo nodded, he said, 'I've heard of it.'

'I can take you in that way.' Hondo looked around at the prisoners who had agreed to stay behind with Hardy. 'You fellers game?'

'Reckon,' said Bowker. 'But we're a mite short on guns and ammo.'

'We'll be leaving ours behind,' Billy

Dysart said. 'Can't risk bein' found with 'em now.'

'They'll do,' Hardy said. 'We can get others from the mustang camp. C'mon. I'll set you boys on the right trail back. And ride easy. There could be patrols this far south already.'

'When we gonna hit the mustang camp?' asked Bowker.

'Tonight — before O'Connor can put 'em on full alert.'

Bowker may have paled a little and his companions moved uneasily. 'Judas, you sure don't waste any time, do you?'

★　★　★

The mustang camp might not yet have been alerted by O'Connor, but there were guards posted just the same. Lying on top of the ridge, looking down on the camp in the pale light of the quarter-moon, Hardy figured this mightn't be as easy as he'd hoped.

There were two short rows of tents down there, four in each row. They were neat, the lines were taut, without sag, and there were no stacks of rifles outside: which meant the guns were in the tents with the soldiers. Off to one side was a banked camp-fire and two shapes in blankets just visible. Likely these were the civilian bronc busters: whether they would fight was something he couldn't know until the lead started flying.

'How many guards you see?' he asked Hondo beside him.

'Three — there, there, and there. But I dunno about them trees between the corral and the spring. It's mighty dark in there and if the officer in charge is as thorough as it looks, there could be another one — or two — back there.'

Hardy agreed. 'Only way to find out is go on down.'

And he started warily down the slope right away. Hondo swore softly, glanced around to see where the other four men were . . . they were sitting on rocks and logs, awaiting orders. Great! Not a bit of initiative among 'em! Gotta be led by the dingus every step of the way!

Hardy was wearing the uniform taken from the battle-crazy man back where Doyle had led the attack on the prison wagon. It fitted tolerably well and the wide-brimmed campaign hat served to keep his face in shadow. He would have preferred moccasins to the heavy army boots, moving about on this gravel, but he set his feet down carefully before putting his weight on them.

Beyond the spring, there was the occasional snort or stomping of the horses in the corrals. The broken ones were closest to the trees but he couldn't yet tell how many. The captured wild ones, yet to feel a hackamore or saddlecloth, were in a separate, heavier corral and they must have sensed him because there was a small racket suddenly erupting from there.

They snorted, whinnied, jostled one another, a couple of cranky mustangs biting, starting a general rough house, making the corral posts creak. Hardy froze, then started moving, figuring he could use the noise to cover his progress.

But the horses' restiveness had flushed two more guards out of the shadows beneath the trees.

Hardy went to ground fast as they stepped out into the light, Spencer carbines at the ready, spreading out as they made their way towards the corrals. This is a well-trained outfit! he allowed silently, even as he moved near to the closest man who had stopped below him.

'See anything, Hank?' the other guard called, his voice giving away his position.

'Somethin's upset 'em!' the man nearest Hardy answered in a harsh whisper. 'We better check it out.'

He started to move away and Hardy jumped, landing a foot behind the startled man, getting an arm around his neck even as the guard started to turn. The man realized instantly he was being choked and triggered his carbine.

The shot shattered the night and really set off the horses now, waking the broken-in ones as well. Through the din, as Hardy choked the man unconscious, snatching his gun, the second guard yelled and came running. No doubt the others were coming, too. In fact, the whole damn camp would be awake after that shot.

The guard spotted Hardy but apparently mistook him for his friend as the light showed his uniform. 'The hell're you doing, Hank? You see something . . . ? *Hell*!'

This last exploded out of the man as he realized it wasn't Hank and he dropped flat even as Hardy triggered the Spencer. The guard fired and Hardy felt the wind of the slug as he levered, cocked the hammer and blasted a second shot one-handed. The guard grunted and slumped and Hardy ran towards the main camp where there was yelling and gunfire.

He slipped twice on the slope, saw the flashes of guns. He heard a man

121

calmly issuing orders to his men and figured it was the officer in charge. A scream of mortal agony rent the night and for an instant all shooting stopped. Then it started again, heavier than before and suddenly a man jumped out of the shadows, grabbed him by the left arm.

'Get over and help Carmody and Logan! Where the hell you comin' from, anyway . . . ?'

Hardy recognized the voice of Sergeant Brick Field at the same time as the man realized Hardy was not one of his men. The redhead jumped back and started to bring up his pistol. Hardy swung the Spencer's iron-bound butt against the side of the sergeant's head and Field collapsed.

He ran to where three soldiers crouched and a fourth lay writhing on the ground. 'All right, boys, time to quit!'

They spun towards him and one started to bring up his rifle but Hardy kicked him in the head. The others dropped their weapons and raised their hands.

'Secured here!' Hardy yelled, and the firing dwindled away and Hondo called, 'Got it under control!'

They had agreed earlier not to mention names, but it wouldn't matter much now that Brick Field was here. He was bound to recognize them.

They rounded up the soldiers, Hardy allowing wounded to be treated. One man was dead, but two more would survive. One of the prisoners had been killed, too.

'All right, drive out the broken broncs,' Hardy told the others. 'Leave the wild ones till we're moving out. They'll cover our tracks.'

'That you, Hardy?' Brick Field sounded groggy, his speech slurred. 'Thought you were in Heaven.'

'Decided it was too much like Hell. We'll be tying you up, Brick, real tight. We need time and we'll take your supplies and ammo, guns and saddles. You'll have a long, thirsty and hungry walk once you leave here, but we'll be long gone by the time you get word to O'Connor.'

'He'll rip the territory apart, stone by stone, till he gets you this time, Hardy. You've already made him look a fool . . . you're a dead man. You just dunno what you're doin', tanglin' with someone like Colonel O'Connor.'

'Mebbe you got that backasswards, redhead,' spoke up Hondo McLane. 'Mebbe it's O'Connor don't realize just what he's doin', tanglin' with Deke Hardy.'

The men moved fast, tying up the soldiers and the two civilian bronc busters who gave no trouble. After the wounded had been treated they, too, were bound hand and foot.

Hardy dragged Field back into the sergeant's tent.

'Brick, you're a hard man, but I reckon you're a halfway decent one just the same — it's Lee. I've got to get her out of that whorehouse.'

Field looked blankly at Hardy.

'Damnit, Brick, you know she shouldn't be there! She's been through enough.'

'The hell you expect me to do about it?'

Hardy's gaze was steady. 'Tell me the lay-out of the place, maybe sketch it, show me the best way to get in — and out again. With Lee.'

'Christ, you don't want much!'

'I've treated your wounded and I've left you alive — so far.'

The redhead glared but muscles were working along his jawline as he thought about that. After a while he said, 'Next time we meet, there won't be any talk, savvy? You just better have a finger on your trigger!'

★　★　★

It was a mighty risky plan but the best Hardy could come up with in the time he had available.

Still dressed in the Yankee uniform, he kept the campaign hat's broad brim pulled low over his eyes as he strolled the boardwalks of Springfield in the early part of the night. Drunks were already staggering out of saloons, leaning against buildings, harassing the citizens and generally making nuisances of themselves.

Hardy walked as casually as he could, now and again giving a little stumble, just to get over the notion that he had had a few drinks himself. He had cleaned up the uniform — and himself, shaving and trimming his hair. He didn't think he would be recognized in the dim light cast by the randomly spaced oil lamps fixed to walls and awnings. A damp wind weaved down the street, clouds scudding across the few stars.

Groups of armed, alert soldiers patrolled the streets closely observing every male civilian, but they barely glanced at men in uniform, so he felt fairly safe for the time being.

He made his way to River Street, seeing the brighter lights down here in the red-light district, hunting the shadows when he could without looking too suspicious. There were groups of soldiers outside the various whorehouses, standing around in packs, drinking from bottles, singing, and laughing over dirty jokes or experiences behind the closed doors of the comfort houses. Hardy made for the one with a bright red door where a group stood noisily, passing around a stone jug of what was probably moonshine. One man grabbed Hardy's arm as he lurched by.

'Frien', you better have a stiff drink if you're a' goin' in . . . Hey! You hear what I said, fellers? A *stiff* drink! I made me a funny . . . '

They laughed and Hardy grinned, took the bottle and had a small swig which he made look a lot bigger. He waved his thanks, exchanged a few bawdy remarks and lurched on down the narrow alley between the cat house and a long building with a sloping roof that he knew would be the goods store

Brick Field had told him about.

Yes, there was the small personnel door in the lower right-hand corner of the larger freight door. He took a slim piece of metal that had been filed to a chisel point from his boot top, worked it beneath the lock plate that held the bolt and padlock and strained the screws loose. He pushed them back in and one dropped out but he left it as he heard footsteps at the street end of the alley.

Swiftly, he thrust the metal into his pocket, fumbled at the front of his trousers and swayed, with his back to the alley mouth.

It was a street patrol and a soldier called, 'What you doin' down there, friend?'

Hardy slurred his words. 'Just shakin' hands with an *old* friend, friend!'

The man chuckled. 'Don't wash the whorehouse away!'

They moved on and Hardy swiftly buttoned up and hurried on down the alley and turned at the corner of the whorehouse. It was a double-storeyed, clapboard building and there was a long ladder resting against the rear wall which was blank except for a single window.

Field — after his initial reluctance — had told him this was for the use of married men who might be visiting one of the ladies and had to leave in a hurry and couldn't use the outside stairway. The window above was false, opened into an empty cupboard inside the building. Hardy wasted no time in going up the ladder, opening the false window and climbing into the musty darkness of the cupboard. He closed the window and eased open the cupboard door an inch. There was a dimly lighted passage outside, the doors of eight rooms visible, four on each side. Field had told him that Lee was stationed in room five, which was actually her prison cell.

She was not allowed to leave the room for any reason and just that thought sent a scalding rage surging through Hardy.

He knew he was entirely in Field's hands now: he had to follow the man's directions, both sketched and verbal, and hope that the redhead hadn't sent him into a trap.

About to step out, he heard men coming up the stairs from the noisy bar room below, eased back, but kept the door open a crack, one hand on the Colt holstered on his left side in the army-favoured crossdraw position, the flap undone.

Two soldiers, one clutching a bottle, weaved into the passage, squinting at the room doors. They stopped, swaying, taking a drink each from the bottle.

'This is it,' one said in a gravelly voice. 'Number five . . . one of them Rebel sluts. Hey, Boone? This the first time you gone two-on-one?'

'Yeah, an' I'm dry-mouthed at the thought!'

The second man snatched the bottle and drank deeply and then the other, laughing, opened the door and staggered inside.

'C'mon, you bitch! Get that dress off an' lessee what you look like!'

It wouldn't have mattered if Colonel O'Connor himself was coming up the stairs with an armed patrol, Hardy could not have restrained himself a moment longer.

He covered the distance to the room so fast that the door was still closing when he reached it. He kicked it violently and charged in. A man yelled as he was propelled across the room, back arched, hat flying, before he smashed face first into the wall. His flailing arms brought down his companion, too, as Hardy closed the door behind him, glimpsed a white-faced Lee crouched on the end of the narrow iron bed in some drab dress. He ran at the soldiers, kicked the man who had slammed into the wall under the jaw and rounded on the second man.

But the soldier cursed and hurled the whiskey bottle at his head. As Hardy ducked, Lee leapt to the door and shot the bolt across and he thought, At least she's still thinking clearly — and then the soldier was coming at him, snatching at his pistol.

Hardy's Colt came up and he shot the soldier in the middle of the chest, the shot loud and hurting his ears in the small room. The man was hurled back and his shoulders smashed through the window and he hung over the sill, unmoving.

Immediately, there was shouting out in the passage and the sound of drumming boots as a group gathered outside Lee's door. Someone banged on the panels with a fist and demanded to know what in hell was going on in there.

Hardy snatched Lee's hand, dragged her off the bed and pushed her towards the broken window. He heaved the dead soldier back into the room and thrust Lee forward. She balked, looking at him wide-eyed.

'Out! Stand on the sill, grab the

gutter and haul yourself on to the roof! *Quick*!' He saw her terror and forced a grin. 'You can do it, Lee! You always were a tomboy!'

She started to climb out, still shaking, and Hardy whirled and put two bullets through the door. There were the sounds of pandemonium out in the passage.

'Gimme that damn shotgun!' a man yelled hoarsely.

Hardy put another shot through the panel, scooped up the pistol belonging to the man he had killed and saw Lee's feet just disappearing past the top of the window. The shotgun blasted and splintered wood, buckshot and gunsmoke swirled into the room. Splinters and lead whistled against the wall near Hardy as he lifted both pistols and triggered at the crowd surging in. Men fell, someone screamed in pain, and then they were swarming out into the passage, a man shouting for someone to put out the goddamn wall lights!

Hardy holstered his empty Colt,

rammed the other gun into his belt and climbed on to the sill. He swung up on to the roof and found Lee crouched just back from the gutter, hands clawed into the shingles, still shaking. He hauled her unceremoniously to her feet and dragged her behind him across the sloping shingles.

Two slid away and he fell but Lee stifled her scream of terror as he floundered up. He hoped all the racket made by the men below in the whorehouse passage would cover any sounds they made crossing the roof. With any luck, they would figure that he and Lee had hung from the window by their hands before dropping into the piled garbage beneath in the alley, then run off into the night.

'Put your arms around my neck!' he panted when they came close to the roof's edge and silently she obeyed.

He felt her thin body stiffen and he increased his pace — then leapt out into space. She screamed softly, mouth buried against his shoulder, as they landed on the roof of the storehouse across the alley. He clawed at the shingles, feeling the splinters go in, dug in with his heels and then had his balance.

The trapdoor in the roof was exactly where Field had drawn it on his sketch and Hardy lowered them both down into the musty loft of the store shed.

'Oh, God, Deke! You've no idea how *hard* I've prayed for you to come!' Lee gasped, clinging tightly to him.

'Not now,' he said curtly and groped eleven paces along beneath the trapdoor, located the ladder he was looking for and guided her down into the main body of the storehouse. It smelled musty and there was a tingling of his nostrils at the odour of spices and carbolic, leather and sacks and coal oil.

Rats scurried away as they made their way through the stacks of goods to the small door in the larger one that led into the alley. Here they crouched for what Hardy judged to be about twenty minutes, listening to the sounds outside as search parties hurried past. He crossed his fingers, hoping no one would stop to rattle the small door to see if it was locked . . . but nothing happened and as the sounds diminished gradually, he gently eased his shoulder against the small door. The steady pressure loosened the screws and they fell out, the padlock dropping with a dull thud to the ground.

Looking out cautiously, he left Lee by the door, groped his way back to the place he had smelled coal oil strongly, found a tin and stabbed his jack-knife blade into the top. It was the oil all right and he splashed it around over the sacks of nearby goods, dropped it on the floor and struck a vesta, quickly closing his eyes against the flare.

By the time he reached the door the sacks were blazing and spilled oil spread snaking flames amongst the other goods. Lee stared at him.

'Diversion — and these are all goods stolen by O'Connor's men in lieu of *taxes* anyway. Let's go, Lee. Hondo's waiting with horses down by the river . . . '

* * *

McLane was there in the darkness of the trees, nervously holding a cocked Spencer rifle across his chest.

'Judas, man, they sound like they're wreckin' the town lookin' for you two!'

'They'll be busier in a minute.'

They mounted and swam their horses across the river and by that time the warehouse was obviously ablaze and lighting up the sky over the town, flames leaping, smoke swirling.

'Hell almighty!' breathed Hondo and there was astonished admiration in his voice. 'You sure got the moves, Deke!'

Hardy turned to Lee who was a good horsewoman, her dress drenched and clinging to her after the river crossing.

'You up to a long ride, Sis?'

She nodded. 'I could ride to Mexico, as long as I leave the — that awful place behind!'

'Good — OK, Hondo, get moving.'

Lee put her horse alongside him as he started to turn his mount. 'Where are you going?' she asked in alarm.

'Got something to do yet — you'll be OK with Hondo.'

'First I knew you wasn't ridin' back with us!' McLane said.

Hardy's face was just visible in the light of the wall of flames reflecting in the river. They could see he was smiling tightly.

'They're gonna be mighty busy with that fire. Seems like a good time to get Flapjack out. *Adios*. I'll see you back at the valley.'

Moments later he was swimming his mount back across the river, away from the reflection of the blaze that was consuming the red-light district of town.

8

Intruder

Deke Hardy didn't realize just how lucky he was.

Word of the mustang theft reached O'Connor a lot sooner than Hardy had thought possible.

Once Brick Field had freed himself, he'd taken two men with him, leaving the others behind at Bedloe Springs to care for the wounded, and had set out across country on foot.

Within hours he had come across a mounted patrol on its way to relieve him so that he could take in the already broken-in horses to Springfield. Some new troops had arrived on the train but they did not have mounts and so these fresh horses were needed urgently.

Field had been given a horse and he

had ridden hell for leather for Springfield, made his report to Colonel O'Connor.

But he had not mentioned that Hardy was planning to rescue his sister from the Red Door whorehouse . . .

He had taken a lot of abuse from O'Connor and had been confined to barracks until further notice. O'Connor had figured out for himself that a man like Hardy would simply have to try to rescue his sister, his only living kin. Accordingly, he'd strengthened town patrols under Lieutenant Chase so that even a cockroach couldn't get through.

But Hardy had struck before this precaution had been fully implemented, although he had seen signs of extra patrols on his way to the whorehouse.

The burning of the goods store had been a piece of fortuitous inspiration . . . the blaze simply could not be ignored, specially in a mainly timber-built town like Springfield. So the search for Hardy and Lee had been called off temporarily while every man

140

in uniform — and all those civilians the Yankees could round up — were sent to the endangered district either to help fight the blaze — which was spreading rapidly — or to help salvage goods from places likely to be threatened.

★　★　★

Hardy had changed into civilian clothes after recrossing the river, stuffing the wet uniform into his saddlebags: it might be required at some future date. He rode around the back of the town, well away from the part that was ablaze, tethered his horse amongst trees not far from the livery. There was no one in the stables when he checked and he took a fresh horse from a stall, a saddle and harness from a peg, swiftly saddled it and took it back to be tethered beside his own mount.

He had two loaded pistols, one in the holster, the second, the one he had taken from the trooper in Lee's room, rammed into his belt.

He knew every step he took was a dangerous one.

The infirmary was at the other end of town to where the fire raged, but everywhere was shrouded with pungent smoke. Hardy tied a kerchief over his lower face like most other people as he made his way towards the rear of the building. There was a deal of activity going on but mostly out the front as injured people or those suffering from smoke inhalation were brought in for treatment. That kept the staff busy and Hardy prowled the quiet, dimly lit passages, looking for Flapjack. He looked into the main infirmary ward, saw the rows of beds, several occupied, some patients at windows watching the drama across town. Hardy figured O'Connor wouldn't keep Flapjack in with the normal army patients, not if he aimed to use him at a later date to help trap Hardy.

He was unfamiliar with the particular lay-out of this infirmary but he had been in others and army builders tended to follow standard plans. 'Private' rooms or rooms where more seriously ill patients could be kept apart from the less urgent cases would be towards the rear where it was quieter.

Once he had to crouch under a bed quickly as two nurses hurried into this section, grabbing armloads of bandages, bowls and ointments for the treatment of incoming patients who had been injured in the fire. When they had gone he made his way into the quieter back section of the building.

Rounding a corner, he stopped dead, tightening his grip on his Colt. There was a soldier at the end of a short hallway, but he had his back to Hardy, was leaning far out the window to get a good look at the fire that painted the night with swirling crimson colours. There was an eeriness over everything, shadows and movement. The man's rifle leaned against the wall but Hardy could see the butt of a pistol in his belt. He moved quietly. There was a lot of noise outside, shouting, the distant crash of collapsing, blazing walls, the movement of horses and wagons. The guard didn't hear a thing behind him and jumped so hard when Hardy touched his shoulder that he crashed his head against the window sill.

White-faced, he spun, belatedly dropping a hand towards his pistol butt. Hardy smashed him to his knees with his Colt barrel, hit the man again across the side of the head and dumped him in the chair by the door. He eased the room door open, wondering if there was a second guard inside, but all he saw was a man propped up on pillows in the usual narrow hospital bed.

'Flapjack?'

The man swung his head around quickly. 'Judas wept!' he breathed. 'I was wonderin' if all that mess out there was mebbe your doin' . . . '

Hardy was beside the bed now. 'You able to ride?'

'Reckon so — if it ain't too rough. I ain't nowhere near as bad as I've been makin' out . . . ' Flapjack was already

144

swinging his legs over the side. He was wearing a long nightgown and was barefoot. 'I ain't got no clothes.'

'Well, looks like you're gonna have to be a Yankee for a spell.' Hardy went outside and dragged in the unconscious guard.

The man's uniform hung loosely on Flapjack's rawboned frame, but he would get by with a little help and the guard's kepi pulled down low over his eyes. He said he was strong enough to carry the man's Spencer rifle so that it would look right if they were seen. He could even cover Hardy as if he was a prisoner if necessary.

Flapjack wasn't as strong as he figured and Hardy had to help him, half-carrying him to where the horses waited. He lifted the wounded man into the saddle, roped him in place to be on the safe side. Mounted, he said, 'Flapjack, we take it easy till we're clear of town, but you gimme a yell if the pace is too much or you're hurting — I mean it. Don't try to bite your lip and suffer in silence. We've a long way to go and once they get that fire out all hell's gonna break loose clear across Missouri when O'Connor starts looking for us.'

'I-I'll be all right.'

'No, goddamnit! Didn't you hear me? Don't suffer in silence! I want you alive. We get caught, they're likely to shoot us on the spot.'

But there had been enough talk and Hardy led the way down to the river . . .

★　★　★

Their luck held and they cleared town without pursuit. Hardy stopped on a small ridge and looked back across the dark miles they had travelled.

There was still a substantial glow in the sky back in the direction of Springfield and he wondered just how much of the town the fire had destroyed — or was *still* destroying.

'They catch us . . . they won't . . . shoot us,' Flapjack said, gritting his words. 'O'Connor'll want to . . . to

146

make examples outa us. He'll hang us.'

'He'll have to catch us first.'

Hardy could tell Flapjack wasn't going to make it without rest. The man's wound had opened up and the uniform tunic was soaked with blood. He was hanging limply from the ropes that held him in the saddle and Hardy made his decision: they were slightly west of Hardyville although the town was several miles beyond the range of mountains that was barely visible because the stars were completely covered by gathering clouds now. There was even thunder and flashes of lightning.

A storm and heavy rain would likely finish Flapjack, so Hardy decided to make for his old place. The house had burned down, but the barn was still standing as far as he knew. He would have to risk taking shelter there while the storm blew itself out, or until daylight anyway. Then he would do what he could for Flapjack and start out once more for the salt pans and the hidden valley beyond.

Flapjack was too far gone to agree or otherwise as Hardy turned towards the ridge, feeling the first drops of rain against his face.

The skies opened suddenly as if slashed by a zigzag streak of lightning that lit up half the countryside. It pelted down, drenching both men in seconds. Hardy wondered if they were getting rain this hard in Springfield: be a pity if it helped put out the fire so soon.

Flapjack was shivering as Hardy led the way through the night, half-blinded by the driving rain. The creeks and rivers would be flooding by morning if this kept up much longer. He would have to cross as many as he could tonight.

By now he was riding alongside Flapjack, supporting the oldster who had passed out completely. It was awkward but he figured they should be arriving at the old ranch any time.

Lightning sizzled and as the resultant thunder boomed and rumbled, Hardy saw the heap of charred timbers that was all that was left of the house. And beyond the sagging, empty corrals, there stood the barn.

He rode straight towards it, in through the open doorway and dismounted, boots squelching, clothes heavy and dripping. He fought to untie the ropes that held Flapjack in the saddle — and then he heard the unmistakable cocking of a gun hammer in the darkness.

'Just lift your hands as high as you can or I'll shoot!' commanded a steady voice.

To add to the surprise that had started his heart pounding, it was the voice of a woman.

★　★　★

Lieutenant Chase was in disgrace.

He had not only allowed Deke Hardy to enter town undetected, but the Reb had rescued his sister and then set fire to the biggest storehouse in Springfield, destroying all the goods O'Connor's men had stolen or taken by force from the citizens of Springfield and surrounding towns. Goods that O'Connor had been aiming to sell selectively, and keep some for himself and perhaps a few others he knew who were not averse to a little graft and corruption.

O'Connor could barely speak as the white-faced lieutenant stood before him, trying not to let his shaking show. He was ashamed that he had slipped up and allowed the disaster to happen, and he knew the only thing he could do was to accept full responsibility.

'Of *course* you must accept full responsibility!' O'Connor roared. 'My hat, man, d'you think there's anyone else to blame?'

'No, sir. But I-I have to say that it's not absolutely certain that it *was* Hardy. I mean the man was in Union uniform and — '

'Get out of my sight! You're confined to barracks until I decide what to do with you. And you might study the manual — the section on digging latrines!' As the crestfallen officer shuffled out of the office, O'Connor shouted, 'And send Sergeant Field in to me at once!'

When Field came in, O'Connor took a moment to recognize him. The man had been fighting the fire which had spread widely through the red-light district of town and he was nearly entirely black, his clothes smelling strongly of smoke and damp. There were burn holes in a dozen or more places and his tufted red hair showed where hot ash had landed. There was a crude, filthy bandage around one hand.

'The colonel wanted to see me, I understand,' he said, snapping to attention, the weariness dragging craggy lines into his face.

'Fire still burning?' O'Connor asked civilly enough after a few moments.

'Yessir. Four comfort houses totally destroyed plus the warehouse and everything in it; two stores fronting River Street gone; a cabin bein' used by an independent whore — and word is she and one or two of her customers didn't get out. There were other casualties — '

'Never mind that,' cut in the colonel. 'You're long overdue for promotion, aren't you, Brick?'

Field blinked, unable to speak for a moment or two, trying to switch his brain from a fire report to this unexpected subject. But he didn't have to reply: O'Connor continued.

'Yes, well, Lieutenant Chase is going to be demoted to the ranks after the utter mess he's made of this night. I'm promoting you — provisionally — to his position.'

Again Field blinked. 'Skippin' the inbetweens, sir?'

'I have the authority to do so if I wish! Do you want the position, Brick? With its attendant rise in pay, naturally.'

'Yes, *sir*! I want it. And — thank you, Colonel.'

O'Connor waved his thanks away. 'The fires are manageable at present?'

'I reckon so, sir.' Field could still not quite believe his promotion. 'The rain's helped get 'em under control.'

'Good. Now I want you to pick some men, the very *best* men — twenty or thirty, say — and I want you to take them and scour the country and bring me back the head of Deke Hardy *and* that slut sister if you wish! But *I want Hardy dead*! Do you understand?'

The redhead nodded slowly. 'He's had a mighty good start, Colonel.'

O'Connor's rage-filled eyes drilled into the new lieutenant's. 'If I was interested in excuses, Brick, I would have left Chase a lieutenant. I said I want you to track down Hardy and the girl. Now pick your men, take whatever you need in the way of guns, ammunition, supplies, spare horses, but get moving before sun-up and *don't come back until you find that son of a bitch*!'

Field nodded. 'Colonel, sir, I'm not makin' excuses, but the storm will have washed out tracks. Some of the rivers might be flooded and we'll have to wait till they drop before — '

He stopped speaking at the murderous look on O'Connor's face. The man was shaking with the rage inside him ready to erupt.

'Just find him, Brick,' he said in a low, steady voice which must have cost him plenty to hold. 'There's a good man. Find Hardy — please?'

Brick Field felt the sweat break out on him anew. By God, the colonel was ten times as scary this way than when he was smashing up the office furniture.

* * *

The woman had lit an oil lamp she had slung on a long rusty nail driven into one of the barn uprights. In fact, Hardy could recall driving that particular nail in years ago, to hang a bridle on for the first horse he had broken in from a mustang for Lee.

Between them, they had got Flapjack off the horse and he was spread out on a blanket now on some musty straw.

154

The woman had made Hardy hand over his guns, including the Spencer carbines and the Blakeslee ammunition boxes. Then she had ordered him to stand back and quite expertly, one-handed she had managed to light the oil lamp.

As she hung it on the nail, Hardy had studied her face: olive-skinned, very dark eyes, slightly tilted, hair so black it gave off deep blue highlights in the lantern's glow. She seemed tall for a woman, but later he noticed she was wearing tooled leather riding boots with heels much higher than usual and he reckoned that without them, she would actually be a mite shorter than average for a woman. She wore a white blouse tucked into the waist of corduroy breeches and there was a small leather holster on the right-hand side of the belt, the pearl handle of a small-calibre pistol showing. He figured it was one of those newfangled Smith & Wessons that used rimfire cartridges. Somehow — he had no real reason for thinking this — but somehow he judged she would know how to use that gun . . .

She had covered him with a Henry repeating rifle and he wondered idly just where she got her firearms. These were the latest available.

'My name is Lisa Rivera,' she told him as they stretched out the unconscious Flapjack, and he heard the touch of accent from south of the Border, or maybe it was Louisiana French: whatever, it was there. 'You are trespassing on my land and while I may not mind giving a man shelter from such a storm, I am not so keen to do so when I find his companion bleeding from a bullet wound.'

'It's an old one, reopened by the ride out here,' Hardy told her curtly. 'And you're wrong: this is not your land. It's *my* land. I built this barn and I grew up in the house which as you've likely seen is no more than a pile of charred timber now.'

Her dark eyes were steady on his face in the light of the lantern and very

156

white teeth tugged lightly at her lower lip. 'You are Deke Hardy?' she asked huskily, and still that trace of accent was audible.

'I'm Hardy. And that old man is a pard of mine, a Texan. We call him Flapjack.'

Her gaze didn't waver. 'You're a wanted man, Mr Hardy — an outlaw. And I understood that — Flapjack — was under armed guard in the Springfield infirmary.'

'He was.'

She waited and when he didn't explain, said quietly, 'And now he lies at my feet, bleeding and unconscious . . . and you brought him here.'

Hardy sighed. 'If that's your way of asking did I break him out, then, yeah, I did. And he needs attention. So can't we sort out this other stuff later?'

'Of course. But you stay well within the circle of light where I can see you and don't move while I examine him.'

Hardy ignored her, knelt beside Flapjack and began working off the wet tunic. The old man groaned and rolled his head. The woman compressed her full lips and watched, still holding the Henry rifle so that it covered Hardy. Gently he rolled Flapjack on to his side so that the wound was visible and he watched her but she did not flinch.

'What can you do for him?' Hardy asked.

'I have a good first-aid kit. I'll get the wound cleaned up and rebandaged. You will allow me to do it, but first I will bind your hands behind your back.'

'You will like hell!'

Then the polished barrel of the Henry rifle flashed through the lamplight like a streak of lightning and next thing he knew after the explosive Fourth of July inside his head, he was down on his knees, with his hands tied together, the end of the rope going around one of the barn's supports.

Lisa Rivera was bending over Flapjack and by the time Hardy's senses cleared, she had rolled the old man on to his back again and covered him with another blanket.

'Got yourself all set up here, I see,' Hardy said, words slurred a little.

He had seen the packing cases she was using as a temporary cupboard, draped with a calico cloth. She had rolled in a tree stump, upended it and was using it as a table. A firepit had been dug in one corner, all straw and anything likely to burn if it caught a stray spark cleared well away. A bedroll was spread out against the wall.

'I intend to live here until I can have the house rebuilt,' she said.

'Lady, if anyone's rebuilding that house, it's me! I told you: this is Hardy land! Always has been.'

'But now you owe much tax to the Reconstruction and to recover it, Colonel O'Connor put your land up for sale just to recover the taxes and some expenses. I bought it and now it is no longer Hardy land: it is Rivera land and I intend to live here, possibly for the rest of my life.'

'That damn O'Connor! He's stolen

most of the county and sold it off! I'd like to know how much of the proceeds the Reconstruction people actually get to see!'

She frowned, eyes glittering as she stared at him. 'You are making dangerous statements, Mr Hardy, but I suppose it matters little — after the crimes you have already committed.'

'Crime — like beauty — is in the eye of the beholder, Miss Rivera.'

'Missus.' She smiled faintly. 'You still have humour despite your situation . . . '

'Well, never mind me for the moment — how is Flapjack? Is he going to be OK? He's tough, but . . . '

'I have done what I can and I think he will be all right.' She glanced past him, out the big doorway. 'I believe the storm is now easing. It will be finished by morning, I think.'

'Then what?'

'Then, we will see.' She looked at him steadily. 'Why did you at first agree to work with O'Connor and then turn against him?'

'I figured I could maybe save some lives if I talked folk around to co-operating. Reconstruction's not right, but it's not going to get any better unless there's give and take on both sides . . . I ought to have remembered O'Connor was a taker, pure and simple. When I saw what had happened to folk I'd known all my life, how they'd been beaten down and still O'Connor wasn't about to ease up, I knew I should never have even listened to him in the first place.'

'So you turned outlaw, risking your life.'

He shrugged. 'I don't think my life was any too secure in any case after I'd *let him down* as he said . . . '

She seemed to think about what he had said, nodded to herself and then moved towards him.

She walked across and he thought she was going to untie him, but instead she only checked that the ropes were knotted securely. The Henry swung towards him as she towered above him, looking down at him soberly, feet spread.

'And when the sun comes up, I think I must take you back to my friend Colonel O'Connor . . . you and the old Texan, Flapjack.' She threw him a strange look. 'But — we see, eh? We will see . . . '

9

Reprisal

Hardy was surprised when the girl agreed to listen to his side of the story.

'You are an outlaw,' she had told him after saying she would have to take him into O'Connor. 'I am new here. I can't afford to have you found on my land . . . '

'*My* land!' Hardy said automatically, and then when she started to protest snapped, 'All right, all right! Leave that for now. Listen, you take me in and they'll hang me. Not to mention Flapjack.'

She looked at the unconscious man briefly. 'I am prepared to care for him. He really can not be moved in safety just now — he can stay here.'

'By himself? While you take me in to O'Connor?'

Lisa Rivera frowned, her eyes smouldering a little. 'You are trying to be smart. Yes, I admit I overlooked that part, but it can still be managed, I think.'

'Mebbe — but it'd be better if you let me go. I got a notion Flapjack'll be all right with you and I'm prepared to accept your word that he can't be moved right now.'

'That's very generous.'

He smiled faintly at her sardonic tone. 'Yeah, ain't it. Look, Lisa, this *is* my land whether O'Connor sold it to you or not. He had no damn right to do it and you know it, deep down.'

'Taxes were owing. It is an accepted way of recovering them. I have seen it many times before.'

'It makes you no better than them white-trash carpetbaggers moving in on cheap land because folk are too dirt-poor to pay.'

Her eyes were really bleak now and to his astonishment he felt a twinge of regret at having spoken so.

'Well, maybe that ain't a real fair comparison, but — well, folks could see it that way.'

'Perhaps I do not care what — *folks* — think about me,' she told him coolly. 'None of this changes the fact that you are a wanted man, Deke Hardy.'

He was silent for a moment. 'S'pose I told you how that came about — would you listen?'

'Ye-es, I would listen. But it may not change my opinion of you.'

'Let's see, eh . . . ?' When she did not object, he briefly told her about the war and its aftermath, with his wandering through Texas, finding the herd of mavericks, rounding them up and driving them to Missouri with the notion of restarting the Hardy spread.

She kept her gaze on his face in the amber light as he told her the rest of the story, leaving nothing out.

'Your . . . sister. That was a terrible thing, placing her in one of those houses. She is — all right?'

'I'm damn anxious to find out.'

165

Lisa frowned. 'You don't know?'

'I sent her back to — somewhere with a friend of mine. It was the best opportunity I'd get to rescue Flapjack, otherwise I would never've done it.'

'You have strong loyalties, I think, Deke Hardy.' Her voice was quiet and thoughtful. 'I think we both need sleep.'

'I'd rather be on my way now the storm's easing.'

'But you forget, I am in command here and I am very tired. We will sleep and I will make my decision in the morning.'

Hardy swore softly and yanked hard at his bonds to no avail. He thought he saw her smile faintly as she turned away.

★ ★ ★

Brick Field didn't feel too good in the stomach as he rapped his knuckles on the front door of the colonel's quarters. He waited, grinding his teeth, hands working, as the tension tightened his stomach muscles.

He could hear O'Connor moving about inside, the rasp of furniture across the flagged floor as the man stumbled into it. Normally, Colonel Kyle O'Connor made his living-quarters in a confiscated house that had once belonged to the town's banker. It was a double-storeyed stone place with portico and columns — and servants. But since the fire and Hardy's escape — not to mention Flapjack being rescued from the infirmary as well — O'Connor had moved back into the best and biggest of the officers' married quarters at the army station. He claimed he wanted to be on hand when news came in that Hardy had been captured.

Now, as he wrenched open the door, hair awry, still tying a robe about his middle, he glared at Brick Field, and then asked, 'Where is he?' His voice was still raspy with sleep.

'Not sure just right now, Colonel, but — '

'My hat, man! You've woken me to tell me you *haven't* found Hardy yet? I specifically told you not to show your face in this town until you *had the man in custody! Or could offer me his head as proof that he was dead!*'

'Colonel, we — '

'Answer my question, damn you!'

The redhead sighed, weary, eyes gritty and sore, his sick belly empty, his body aching from long, long hours in the saddle, drenched through from the rain.

'Colonel, I'm tryin' to explain.'

O'Connor made a production of looking around the bleak early morning parade ground, up and down the building where his quarters were. 'I do not see Deke Hardy, nor that smelly old Texan. So what is there to explain, Brick!'

His voice was menacing and he spoke through gritted teeth, the anger rising in him. Field tried once more.

'I think we can get him before sundown, Colonel.' He paused but

O'Connor's bleak face lost none of its frostiness as he waited for Field to continue. 'I have men out now and with a little luck — '

'*Luck!* My hat, man, don't talk to me about *luck!* This requires *effort* and team work — and, goddamn it, some show of common sense and perseverance. Now, you get back out there wherever you've been and this time *do not return until you have found Hardy!*' His voice dropped back to normal, and in an almost friendly tone, he added, 'Now there's nothing hard in understanding those orders, is there, Brick?'

'No, sir, but if I could just — '

'Just follow your orders, that's the best thing you can do, Brick. Do you understand that? The very best thing you can do!'

The door started to close. 'It's your reprisals, Colonel!' the redhead almost shouted and the door paused, the colonel's pale face glaring at him through the opening.

'What about them?'

O'Connor had been in such a rage after Hardy's escape and rescue of both his sister and Flapjack, as well as burning a good portion of the town, that he had decided reprisals were in order. Pausing in his anger, O'Connor had smiled. 'Hardy seems to enjoy burning things, so burn a few of their ranches. Shoot anyone who resists and I mean *anyone*, be it man, woman or child. Confiscate their food and money. Kill their stock and make them butcher it for the army's kitchen. Tear down fences, burn pastures, string up a few damn Rebels and let them swing in the breeze with a shoot-to-kill order on anyone who attempts to cut down the corpses. Turn the men loose throughout the county, and then — then tell them they have Deke Hardy to blame for it all! Then someone might turn him in, or even co-operate with us.'

It had been a reign of terror and it had subdued the people like nothing else had to date. But there was a new

170

sullenness as well. Folk might know they couldn't resist this kind of terror campaign, but they *could* bide their time — which, actually, was the only option open to them — and one day there would be an opportunity sooner or later for resistance or, better still, a real fight back.

Meantime, they would endure what they had to.

Or some of them would. Others would decide they had had enough and move out.

Bernie Doyle was one of these. He was a family man, already disadvantaged by having had his property stolen and, with nowhere to go, being taken in by Dal Gilbert and Billy Dysart, moving his family back and forth between the houses.

'This is too much for me,' Bernie announced after supper, when he and Dysart were nursing fresh injuries received from beatings given by the soldiers that afternoon. 'Where's it gonna end? With all of us dead, or wishin' we were. I'm gettin' out.'

They all looked at him as if he was crazy.

'Gettin' out is a good idea,' slurred Dysart through swollen lips and broken teeth. 'But where the hell can we go?'

Doyle gave him a steady look. 'To that valley where Deke's set up his hideout. It's lush and hidden away. We could all homestead it for a spell, till this damn Reconstruction's over — if it ever *is* over.'

'Hell, Bernie, that's a good place, but — you mean lock, stock and barrel?'

'None of us have *any* locks, stocks *or* barrels. Billy! We go with what we're wearin' and what we can carry. An' we go *now*. No talkin' it over, no meetin's to discuss it — it's the only thing to do and me an' my family's doin' it. You and Dal are welcome to come along, but don't stay one more day, or the only way any of us'll leave is in a coffin . . . '

Field, of course, knew nothing about such a conversation, but he *did* know the Doyles, Dysarts and Gilberts had quit town, separated, moving off in three different directions.

'Then drag them back!' roared O'Connor when the redhead told him it at the door of his quarters. 'Drag them back and bring them before me! I'll make such a damn example of them that no one else will dare try it!'

'Colonel, I've got my best teams watchin' 'em and it looks very much as if they're all makin' for the same place although they've tried to make us think they were goin' their separate ways.'

'Then they'll be so much easier to grab — '

'Sir, why nab them? Why not *follow* them?' Brick's heart was hammering as he put his idea to the colonel. 'There's only one place they'd be goin' together . . . to join Hardy! We follow and we get them all.'

It took O'Connor less than three seconds to see the value of Field's suggestion and he smiled. 'Knew it was the right notion to promote you, Brick.'

He grinned, then swung open the door. 'Come on in. Have some breakfast with me, and soon as your men report in — how are they going to do this, by the by, without risking losing Hardy meantime?'

For the first time since the notion had formed in his head that morning, Brick Field smiled.

'They're equipped with heliographs, sir.'

O'Connor stared at him, then smiled too. 'Ah!' he said.

★　★　★

Hardy hadn't been back in the hidden valley for more than an hour when he realized that Lee was not a happy woman. Sure, she had laughed and smiled when he had returned, thrown her arms about his neck and hugged him in welcome.

But he knew her moods and he saw she was holding herself in, putting on a face, making the best of things when,

174

really, she was way down in a depressed state.

Bowker and Hondo McLane had told him that on her return, still worried about the fate of Hardy and Flapjack, she had kept to herself and later gone down to a remote pool that Hondo had shown her, displaying a depth of understanding for Lee's feelings that Hardy would never have guessed at.

There she had scrubbed her skin almost raw with handfuls of sand, washed her hair over and over with leaves from the soap bush, crushed flowers and aromatic leaves and rubbed their juices all over her body. Then she had put on the faded and worn clothes Hardy had left for her: cut down trousers and shirt, a pair of moccasins he had made for her.

She spoke when spoken to, but volunteered little, forced herself to do some camp chores, aware of the uncomfortable stares of the men, wishing that Hardy would return. There was a smooth boulder down at the creek's edge that she favoured, and she sat there for hours with her knees drawn up, her arms wrapped around them, staring unfocused into space.

Hardy took some coffee down there, sat beside her and although she glanced at him he knew she hadn't really seen him.

'Told you there's a woman living on our land, sold to her by O'Connor. Strange type. Part Mexican or maybe New Orleans French . . . confident and seems efficient. Says she's Mrs Rivera but let slip she's a widow. She was gonna turn me in but for some reason changed her mind overnight. Taking care of Flapjack now . . .'

'I hope he'll be all right,' Lee said dully, not really interested.

He rolled a cigarette, made a couple more attempts at conversation but got nowhere. He decided to take the bit between his teeth instead of fooling around.

'You're free of that place now, Lee.

You don't have to worry about going back there, ever — you have my word.'

Slowly, she turned her dulled eyes towards him. 'I'm not worried about going back. I know I'll never do that — I'll kill myself first.'

'Hey, sis, come *on!*' It shook Hardy some, for he knew when she really meant something or was merely talking.

'Deke, don't you understand? I'm so — *ashamed*! You have no *idea* what I had to do in that place! It was — ' She almost choked on the memory and for a moment he thought she was actually going to throw up. But she recovered, sobbed once, dry-eyed, staring out across the creek now. 'The things I *did* . . . I'll never be able to forget them, Deke. *Never!*'

He slid an arm about her shoulders, but they were stiff and resisting. 'Lee, it wasn't what you *did* — it was what you had to *endure*. Christ, Sis, you were the *victim*! You did what you were told or they'd have killed you.'

'At least there would've been

oblivion! An end!'

He shook her briefly. 'Now stop that! It's stupid talk! You were a prisoner and you did what you had to to survive. It kept you alive long enough for me to come and break you out — and that's the important thing, Lee. You're out now, free, safe. That's how you have to think about it, put the rest behind you. It won't be easy, but you can do it, you've always been strong-willed.' He put some lightness into his voice. 'Hell, I've got reason to know that — the way you ran things after Ma died! You had Pa and me and the other boys running around in circles, afraid to even walk in the house with our boots on and — '

Suddenly her shoulders were shaking violently and she was crying, real tears now, turning towards him, clinging to him, sobbing out all the hurt and the guilt. He held her, stroking her hair gently, knowing that it was going to be all right now: it would still take time, but she was going to get over this and one day soon he would have his laughing sister back.

It was something to look forward to.

Then, Jimmy Durango, one of the prisoners who had escaped from the wagon with Hardy, and who had been on watch at the entrance to the valley, called down from his outpost, 'Someone comin'! A whole slew of 'em!'

10

Cornered

They were all ready for a fight and were vastly relieved when Jimmy Durango called down again.

'It's folks, is all!'

'What 'folks'?' rapped Hardy, crouching behind a rock with his Spencer at the ready, thumb on the big hammer spur. Lee hunkered down beside him, tightlipped, holding a pistol confidently.

'Folks from town, looks like,' answered Durango. 'Bernie Doyle — an' I reckon his missus and two gals. Billy Dysart and there's no mistakin' Dal Gilbert with his one arm — and his missus, too, and their kids! Judas, we runnin' a family picnic or what?'

'Stay put, Jimmy,' Hardy said, standing now, the carbine down at his side. 'Just make sure no one followed them.'

No one was too disappointed it wasn't an attack by the Yankees but they were all puzzled as the riders drifted down into the valley from the rim.

'I wonder what's happened?' Lee mused. 'I mean, why would they all come out here?'

'We'll soon find out,' replied Hardy as he walked forward to meet little Bernie Doyle as the man dismounted. They shook hands gravely. Hardy touched a hand to his hatbrim in Mrs Doyle's direction, winked at the young girls.

Billy Dysart tossed him a casual salute as he loosened the cinchstrap on his alkali-coated mount. Its head was hanging and it was obviously weary. Dal Gilbert's horses also were showing sign of strain. Lee was already talking with Sarah Gilbert quite animatedly.

The men and Hardy walked back to where the others waited, Hondo McLane thumbing his hat to the back of his head.

'Man, we got us a ready-made community!' he breathed.

Bernie Doyle looked at him sharply. 'You might be righter than you know, Hondo.' He turned to Hardy. 'O'Connor's made the whole county a true hell, Deke — since that fire and you gettin' out with Lee and old Flapjack.' He glanced around. 'Where is he by the by?'

'My old place. There's a woman named Rivera taking care of him.'

'Who the hell is *that*?' asked Dysart, as the others looked curiously at Hardy.

He told them briefly of his rescue of Flapjack and the storm and how the old Texan's partly healed wound in his back had reopened. 'She seems all right,' he concluded. 'I don't like her being on my place but she's got it legal as far as Reconstruction law is concerned and there's nothing I can do about it right now. But I believe she'll take good care of Flapjack.'

Dysart stroked his stubble. 'Well, I hope so. If she's had dealin's with

O'Connor, though . . . '

'Never mind her,' Hardy cut in. 'Why did you folk come here?' He set a sober gaze on Bernie Doyle. 'Ever think you might be followed?'

'Sure. That's why we left town separately, met up again at the salt pans. The storm the other night had flooded 'em, made 'em too boggy to cross. We had to go all the way around 'em, which is what took us so long to get here.'

Hardy frowned. 'Hell, Bernie you could've left tracks coming through all those draws and gulches with all that silt in their bottoms!'

Doyle's gaze narrowed. 'If we did, we wiped 'em out. The hell kinda fool you take me for, Deke?'

Hardy held up a placating hand. 'All right — long as you're sure. And now you're here we'll all pitch in and get some shelters for the womenfolk. Hope you brought your guns!'

Doyle smiled faintly, but a little reluctantly. He had the small man's touchiness and he didn't like anyone thinking he might have been sloppy and left a trail for O'Connor's men to follow.

'Yeah, we brought our guns — all taken apart and scattered about our persons and gear. Just in case we was stopped.'

He looked challengingly at Hardy.

'Sounds like a right smart move,' Hardy said and saw Doyle relax.

Which was good — no sense in causing dissension now.

'OK, you can go into detail while we start cutting some of those saplings yonder. Jimmy! You keep your eyes open up there!'

Happy-go-lucky Jimmy Durango waved, settling his back comfortably against a sloping boulder, folding his hands across his chest as he looked out over the heat-pulsing flats to the distant salt pans. Slowly, his eyes closed.

★ ★ ★

Lisa Rivera was horrified when Colonel Kyle O'Connor told her that he was going to hang Flapjack.

'But you can't!' she protested, rising from her chair and leaning on the front of the Union officer's desk, her golden skin losing a little of its colour. 'He's a sick man! He needs urgent medical attention, the way his wound is haemorrhaging! That's why I brought him into town!'

O'Connor raised his eyes to her handsome but shocked and angry face. 'You'd have done better to bring him the moment he — er — wandered into your barn, my dear.'

'There was a storm! You know how severe it was. He came into the barn, slumped in the saddle, the wound bleeding profusely. I had no thought about who he might be or whether he was law-abiding or not. I saw he needed help and I did what I could for him. But now he's taken a turn for the worse and as the doctor in Hardyville was too drunk to do anything, I hired a buckboard and brought him here.'

'Yes, yes, most commendable and humane — but it doesn't change the fact that he is an escaped outlaw, a murderer. He *was* alone, wasn't he? There wasn't another man with him, Deke Hardy by name?'

Lisa looked steadily at the colonel. 'He rode in alone. I saw no one else and he hasn't mentioned anyone. But, surely, Colonel, you aren't serious about hanging that old man! I mean, it would be cruel to nurse him through his wounds just to send him to the gallows!'

O'Connor pursed his lips. 'Yes, I suppose it would.' He smiled warmly. 'No, I won't do that.'

She looked relieved and sat down in her chair again. 'I'm glad to know that, Colonel . . . I have been hearing such — disturbing talk about the way your men have been acting. Killing, raping, plundering, burning — they seem to be rampaging through the countryside like a band of . . . Vikings!'

The colonel gave his shoulders a slight shrug. 'I can understand them being infuriated by Hardy's actions. After all, they, too, will have to go hungry now that Hardy burned the storehouse . . . and staying in town while we fought the fire just so he could break out that smelly old Texan — well, my dear, it's tantamount to his thumbing his nose at the Union and *none* of us is prepared to allow that.'

Her dark eyes held his steadily. 'The way I heard it, they were acting on orders from you, Colonel.'

He arched his eyebrows. 'Is that what you heard? Well, that, too, is understandable, that these Rebels would think that.'

'Surely they aren't rebels now, Colonel — the war is over . . . '

He looked surprised at her words. 'I believe I know that, Mrs Rivera! You do not need to teach me to suck eggs and I must point out that *you* are liable for prosecution because of your aiding and succouring a known outlaw. Actually

187

you are in a very serious position. It is up to me to decide if I should proceed with charges against you or not . . . '

'So I had best watch my step, I think,' she said, forcing a tight smile. 'Yes, I see your position, Colonel, and I'm sure you understand my motives were strictly humanitarian.'

'Yes, I believe that. It is all, in fact, that has saved you from prosecution . . . but nothing can save the old Texan.'

She blanched and opened her mouth to speak but the door opened and O'Connor snapped his hot gaze towards it, ready to cuss-out the intruder. But before he could say anything, Acting-Lieutenant Brick Field, dishevelled and sweaty, clinging to the edge of the office door, gasped, 'The heliographs, Colonel! Just flashed through a message. They've located Hardy and a-a bunch of Rebs . . . I'm gathering men now . . . '

O'Connor was on his feet. 'I'll come with you! I want to see the end of Mr Deke Hardy. If he lives through the attack, he'll swing.' He shot his gaze side-long at the woman. 'Right along-side his friend, Flapjack!'

She gasped, rose quickly. 'You can't — you can't mean you're going to hang that old man anyway! He's probably dying.'

'Then we shall put him out of his misery.'

'But he may not live long enough to stand trial!'

'Oh, there's no question of a trial,' O'Connor told her with a crooked grin, buckling on his pistol and sword belt over his tunic. 'He was wanted for the murder of my men in a cattle stampede he helped instigate. He escaped custody — which is a hanging offence in itself.' He turned to Field who was recovering his breath now. 'We'll leave right after the execution.'

Lisa Rivera swayed and sat down heavily as Kyle O'Connor jammed his hat on his head and smiled as he walked out of his office, Field holding the door open for him.

* ★ ★

Out in the hidden valley, things were happier.

They had a small welcoming party for Bernie Doyle and the others. Life had been pretty damn miserable for so long that Hardy figured it was worth taking a chance so they could relax some, ease the tensions they had all been living with since Appomattox.

Jimmy Durango was relieved after dark and Tom Bates who climbed up to the lookout had to wake him up.

'Damn it, Jimmy! You were s'posed to be watchin' in case Doyle and his friends had been followed! Hardy'll beat your head in, he finds out you been sleepin'.'

Durango stretched and yawned. 'He won't if you don't tell him, Tom. Then I won't have to tell him how you watched his sister wash-up in that pool.'

Bates swore. 'Hell, that's all I done — just look. All right, go get your grub. I won't say nothin'.'

190

Durango grinned. 'Now don't you be dozin' off, Tom!' he said with a laugh as he started to climb down.

Hondo McLane had shot a deer earlier, before the arrival of the folk from Hardyville, and the venison cooking over the fire pit filled the valley with appetizing odours. There were wild onions and thyme and sage and some potato-like tubers and wild honey to go with the camp bread Bowker had baked in the coals.

Billy Dysart had a battered har-monica and played songs of the old South and they sang along. Hardy watched Lee closely and slowly, as the evening progressed, he saw her truly relaxing. Her smiles were wider and less forced. The laughter came naturally and she even did an imitation of a sailor's hornpipe she had seen at a snake-oil show that had visited Hardyville before the war. The group clapped and although there was no booze to loosen inhibitions everyone had a mighty fine time.

Hardy reckoned things had only really got going after Tom Bates had gone to relieve Jimmy Durango and he figured he ought to let Bates join in. Hardy had had plenty to eat, had enjoyed the party but had never been one for prolonged celebrations. He didn't want to wind it down just yet so climbed to the lookout to relieve Bates. The man was sitting against a rock, facing out across the flats, only a grey blur in the starlight although the edge of the rising moon was showing above the ridge to the north-east.

'Tom, go on down and fill your belly with some of that venison — Mrs Doyle took over the cooking chores and it's a mighty big improvement on Hondo's efforts . . . Tom! Damnit, man. You sleeping?'

'No he ain't sleepin' — he's dead!' said a deep voice in the shadows behind him. 'Just like you're gonna be!'

Hardy had spun at the first word, glimpsed the Yankee soldier coming at him with the naked bayonet, held low down, angled upwards to rip open his belly and go on and pierce his vital chest organs.

Hardy jumped aside, hit the man's bayonet arm, kicking at his leg. The soldier grunted, fell against a rock. Hardy was on him in a flash, smashing his face into the granite. The man sagged, but he was game, twisted around, and the bayonet ripped Hardy's sleeve and opened a gash in his arm. He wrenched the weapon free, quickly reversed it and drove it into the man's chest, clapping a hand over his mouth, stifling the scream.

Breathing hard, he lowered the man to the ground, swiftly checked Tom Bates. He was dead, all right. Hardy had his six-gun in his hand now, crouched, straining to see over the flats. He *thought* there was something moving out there, something a little more solid and darker than the greyness.

His ears picked up the slight creak

and jingle of harness gear, the clink of a hoof.

It was enough. He clambered down swiftly into the valley and ran for the camp where they were cheering Bowker and Hondo who were prancing about in some kind of improvised dance. They stopped as Hardy burst in and kicked at the fire, scattering the burning wood.

'Yankees!' he panted. 'They've killed Tom Bates and there looks to be a whole troop moving in.'

They stared at him dumbly — then abruptly scattered.

There was no need to order anyone to grab their guns.

Since they had taken all the firearms from Brick Field's mustang camp, there were enough for the women too, and, white-faced, they took the weapons from their men who quickly showed them how to work the Spencer carbines.

'Try to save ammo,' Hardy told them, watching the valley entrance. 'We don't have a lot to spare. Kids, you ever made paper cartridges for your pa . . . ?'

He soon had the children making up paper cartridges for the six-guns, using an empty Spencer cartridge case as a powder measure.

Then Hardy was running for the lookout again, spreading out his men. He was halfway to the top when the first of the Yankees rode down the ramp into the far end of the valley. They were spreading out in disciplined order and he thought he heard O'Connor's voice as well as Brick Field's.

No sense in hesitating any longer, he figured, and he settled himself on a small ledge, lifted his rifle and aimed at the dark shapes of men, now on foot, hunting cover. He found a small group, doubled-over as they ran towards the creek, likely aiming to walk up it to the camp. The Spencer thudded against his shoulder as he worked the lever, manually cocked the hammer each time. But while the gun wasn't as fast as a Henry repeater where the levering action also cocked the hammer, Hardy got off five shots very quickly and three men went down, splashing. Another stumbled and the remaining two men had white water foaming against their legs as they waded wildly in an attempt to get around the bend. One of them might have made it — one definitely didn't.

Hardy dropped behind a rock an instant before a dozen guns opened up and raked the general area around him. They must have been shooting at his gunflash, hadn't actually seen him — yet.

He dropped down several feet, jarring his body, sprawling on a stony patch between two boulders. He got off his last two shots from the Spencer, opened the butt plate, withdrew the spring, pushed in the tin tube from his Blakeslee holder, filling the butt-stock magazine with seven more .52 calibre cartridges. Quickly he compressed the spring.

He was firing seconds later, picking off a man who was zigzagging as he ran towards the foot of the steep slope that led to the lookout. The man somersaulted. Then others found his position and sent a hail of lead in his direction. He lay flat, pressing against the stones, hearing the thunderous noise as gunfire filled the entire valley.

He judged O'Connor had at least thirty, maybe forty men, and his heart sank.

They couldn't hold out against such numbers for long. No doubt there would be reinforcements coming, too.

Then the gunfire dwindled and Brick Field's voice drifted down through the cloud of gunsmoke.

'Hardy! You can see you're in a helluva fix! We've got more men blocking the other end of the ravine, so there's no escape. We don't want to harm the women and kids so show some sense and surrender now!'

Field waited. Hardy waited in silence. Then there came a ragged volley from behind the camp where his own men were scattered about the rocks.

'There's your answer, Brick!' Hardy called, rolling swiftly to his left, throwing himself down the slope. And just as well he did — a dozen guns raked the spot where he had called from. He smiled thinly: Field was smart, had his sharp-shooters all ready for when he had answered. It had been a risk but he had pulled it off — and now he knew just how serious they were.

O'Connor was going to finish this tonight, kill them all while he had them cornered.

By then the gunfire had increased again and the small valley was filled with snarling sounds like a swarm of maddened bees. Lead ricocheted everywhere, showering Hardy with rockdust as he rolled again, shooting his carbine across his chest at the shape of a man clambering over the rocks above, trying to come up on him from behind while others kept him busy. The man dropped from sight but Hardy didn't think he'd hit him.

Two more shapes came pounding in across from the left and he rose to one knee, led one slightly and blew him off his feet. The second man swerved, triggered a six-gun wildly, having no chance of finding target, merely shooting as a diversion. Hardy shot his leg out from under him and the man screamed as the heavy bullet shattered the bone and he tumbled in behind a deadfall, sobbing out that he needed a medic.

No one moved towards him and he began to curse his own comrades.

Field sent in four more men from the left, six from the right.

Hardy emptied the Spencer, moved quickly as lead hummed around him, kicking gravel into his face, tearing lines of dust from the boulders. Panting, he crawled under more rocks, deep into the boulder field at the base of the cliff. Between shots he listened for his own men, heard the guns banging raggedly, wondering how long the ammunition was going to last.

He had no chance of getting to the camp now where he hoped the kids were keeping their heads down and had a good stack of pistol cartridges ready. He loaded his last Blakeslee tube into the Spencer's butt magazine and crawled on his belly, using elbows and knees to make his way through the rocks. Soldiers were shouting, but he couldn't make out what they were saying, his ears were ringing so wildly from all the gunfire.

He reached the edge of the rocks and there was an open space of several yards before the next line of boulders. They would have their rifles trained on that pale patch, he figured, awkwardly turned around and coughed as a probing ball filled his mouth with sand. He flattened as a tighter volley raked his shelter immediately, but then he was moving again, back to the other side. He hoped most of the soldiers were watching that empty patch of gravel, waiting for him.

Then he came up behind a bush

growing at the edge of the rocks. He could see the stars gleaming in the creek twenty yards away. There were no signs of Yankees but it didn't mean they weren't watching it. They had plenty of men to watch almost every square foot of the valley! he thought bitterly, gathered himself and lunged for the creekbank.

He weaved across the ground, jumping from rock to rock. A single rifle banged and his hat was whipped from his head.

Sharpshooter! he thought. They'd posted a sharpshooter to watch the creek. And the man fired again and Hardy felt the tug of a ball at his shirtsleeve. His arm was already burning from the bayonet gash and he wasn't sure if the ball touched his flesh or not. But then the creek was within reach and he plunged in, turning sharply, throwing the sniper's aim, hearing the ball *thrum* over his head. He dropped, rolled on to his back — and saw the man had stood up from his cover behind a big deadfall so as to get a better shot.

He found Hardy immediately, swung his rifle around, as Hardy brought up the Spencer, water dripping from it. As he thumbed back the hammer, he hoped it wouldn't misfire and the guns thundered together. But it was the sharpshooter who reared up on to his toes, head snapping back violently, before he spilled awkwardly across the rocks. The man's bullet ripped into the shallows beside Hardy who was now up and running, water splashing in a fan.

Someone shouted and bullets made ragged spouts all about him and then he threw himself bodily around the bend, went under, gulped, floundered back into the shallows and, staggering, lunged up into the brush, making for the campsite.

Hondo almost shot him as he fell into the camp, breathless, bloody sleeve dangling, hatless and wild-eyed.

'Cover . . . the . . . creek!' Hardy gasped and Hondo nodded, moved away to do just that, his gun starting to fire.

Lee turned a white, powder-streaked face towards him, gave him a quick smile and started to reload her rifle. The other women were shooting, too, and Hardy groaned: they were firing wild, wasting ammunition . . . but he saw that it was too late now.

They were almost out. The children, frightened but game, had no more powder to make into paper cartridges and he saw that most of the paper rolls were too uneven to fit into a six-gun's chamber easily. The bulges would burst and the powder would be lost, causing misfires or loss of power behind the balls. But he grinned at them, tousling the hair of the Gilbert boy.

'You did fine, kids! Real fine! Now leave it and get back under cover — *Go*!'

Mrs Gilbert looked at him but he said nothing, ran to the crouching Bowker who had a bloody face and was working his gun one-handed.

'I'm OK,' the man said. 'They got Jimmy Durango, though, smack through the middle of the forehead.'

'Anyone else?' Hardy asked tightly.

'Billy got his arm broke by a ball and I think Dal got himself a scalp-burn. Deke, we're in lousy shape, *amigo*. Low on ammo an' I'm scared for the women and kids . . . '

So was Hardy.

He made his decision, knowing they were going to be out of ammunition — they were unable to use many of the cartridges the children had made.

He gathered up a handful of the paper rolls of powder, grinned at the kids and tore open the ends of a half-dozen tubes before throwing them into the small pile of embers that was all that remained of the fire.

There was a huge *whooosh!* a column of flame jumping six feet high, half blinding them all.

As he had hoped, the Yankee firing ceased, as they wondered what had happened at the camp. Hardy called into the brief silence and the dwindling echoes of gunfire.

'O'Connor! Call off your dogs — we're willing to go down fighting but you have to let the women and children out.'

The women immediately protested, but the men backed Hardy. Then when they saw the pale, frightened faces of the children, the women's arguments faded slowly.

'It's the only way,' Hardy told them. 'We're almost out of ammunition.' He looked around at the men and without exception, they nodded: they would go down fighting.

'Think we can trust O'Connor?' asked Hondo sceptically.

'Have to . . .'

But it was Brick Field who finally answered: apparently O'Connor still considered it beneath his dignity to shout in any kind of a parley.

'Colonel agrees, Hardy. The women and kids can go unharmed. Provided you and your men throw out your guns first.'

'Oh-oh!' murmured Bernie Doyle. 'Don't like the sounds of that!'

'Just let them go,' called Hardy. 'We'll take our chances.'

'No! Fightin's done. You lost, and you want to save your womenfolk, do like we say — or no deal!'

It was hard to make out all the faces around him but Hardy thought that all the men finally nodded agreement: there was no choice, really.

'All right!' he called, throwing his Spencer into the night by the barrel. 'We're coming out. One by one . . . '

'No, dammit!' hissed Bowker, coming quickly to where Hardy was standing and hauling him down again. Despite his wound, Bowker was strong and he was angry.

He rolled on top of Hardy and pinned him by sheer weight — plus the fact that Hardy was reluctant to slug the man when he was bleeding so much from his head wound.

'It's the only thing to do, Bowker!' Hardy gritted, starting now to fight the grip. 'We've got to give the women and kids a chance. Even if they're not your women and kids.'

'With O'Connor?' Bowker gritted, his strength gradually giving way as Hardy put on more pressure, pushing up the man's arms slowly but inevitably. 'You can't trust a son of a bitch like that!'

'There's no blamed *choice*!'

Hardy threw the man off him and then wondered why the others hadn't hauled Bowker off before this. He frowned, looking around, saw they were still holding their weapons.

'What's this? I thought we agreed that the women and kids . . . '

'Have to have their chance, yeah,' cut in Dysart. '*They* can walk out, Deke; we aim to go down fightin'. O'Connor's gonna kill us anyway.'

The womenfolk again started protesting, running to their men, the children crying now. Lee stood to one side, her teeth tugging at her lower lip. But her gaze was on Hardy.

He saw her and spread his hands as he stood, querying with arched eyebrows. Lee shook her head, indicating she didn't know what he should do.

That makes two of us, Hardy thought grimly.

Tight-lipped Hardy turned to the others when Brick Field's voice reached him.

'We're waitin,' Hardy! Guns first, then the women and kids can go . . . while you stand around with your hands in the air and watch 'em.'

He paused and when there was no immediate reply, called more harshly, 'You savvy what I'm sayin'? And this is the *last* time I do say it: *throw out your guns!* All of 'em! Then come on out, hands in the air. The only other option is to stay put — while we charge! And you know about our cavalry charges: once they get under way it's no mercy!' Colonel says he'll give you thirty seconds to make up your mind.'

'Not even O'Connor would slaughter

women and kids!' growled Bernie Doyle, but there was uncertainty in his voice.

And, as Hardy started to try to talk some sense into them, he saw the uncertainty on the men's faces, too.

'Time's ticking away, gents,' he said quietly.

It was the first distant shout of '*Mount!*' that finally stirred the outlaws.

'Christ, they're gonna do it!' breathed someone and then the guns began to be thrown out into the night and the women sobbed.

Whether in joy, pain or relief, Hardy couldn't tell.

But this time, no one tried to stop him when he lifted his hands and stepped out towards the enemy.

11

Last Sunrise

The survivors were standing in a group, their hands bound behind them. Soldiers with bayonets fixed stood guard, and looked as if they wanted to use their weapons.

Hardy and his men tried to close their ears to the sounds of gunshots coming from where they had left the wounded.

The colonel smiled at Hardy, watching his face intently in the firelight. 'I vowed no prisoners today, Deke, under the circumstances. Well, you know how it is. But it won't trouble you for long. You or your friends.'

Hardy tensed and Mrs Dysart heard the colonel's words and tried to run to her man but was restrained roughly by two soldiers.

'No!' she cried in horror, having immediately divined the officer's meaning. A hard hand clamped over her mouth and she was hauled away with the others, the children starting to cry as they were hustled along.

Brick Field stepped in when a soldier threw Lee to the ground as she tried to fight free of his grip. The man lifted his rifle butt, but Field shoved him back roughly. Brick's tunic was undone and there was a crude bandage around his lower ribs where he had apparently been slightly wounded in the gunfight.

He helped Lee to her feet and she fell against him, in close. Then she snapped her head up, stepped back quickly against his grip, staring into his face with something like horror. Hardy saw it and frowned in puzzlement. Field's face, too, was bewildered as the girl flung herself away from him only to be taken by the arm by another soldier.

Field frowned as she was led off. Lee stared at her brother, a strange fear on her face, but she said nothing.

'Where are they being taken?' Hardy rasped.

Colonel O'Connor regarded him coldly. 'You are not in any position to ask questions, Deke, but I'm feeling generous so I'll answer you. They are all being returned to Springfield. I — er — may want to question them later.'

Hardy tore free of the men holding him, rammed the top of his head into O'Connor's smug face. The colonel gasped and gagged as he staggered back, went down to one knee, his nose broken, blood flooding over his chin. Brick Field clubbed Hardy to his knees with his pistol butt, helped O'Connor shakily to his feet, fumbling out a kerchief. But the colonel pushed it aside, preferring to use one of his own, holding it over his bleeding nose and mouth, eyes blazing at the groggy Hardy.

'As soon as it's light enough to see, hang him!' he ordered in muffled tones. He raked the others with his bleak eyes. 'Hang all of the Rebel scum!'

'Yessir,' Field said a little tightly, ordering two men to get the doctor up here right away to attend to Colonel O'Connor.

'Double-crossing bastard!' snapped Hardy as O'Connor stumbled away. He swung towards Field. 'What about the kids?'

'They'll be all right,' the redhead told him. 'Whatever happens to 'em ain't gonna bother you, Hardy. You're a fool. He might not have hung you if you'd had enough sense to throw a hitch on that temper of yours.'

Hardy scoffed. 'He aimed to string us up all along.'

'Well, you surrendered.'

'I thought — hoped — it might at least save the womenfolk and those kids. But I ought to've known O'Connor wouldn't keep his word. The others tried to warn me . . . '

'The kids won't be harmed — he ain't that stupid.'

'He hung poor old Flapjack. That was pretty stupid!'

Field looked at him. 'None of this is gonna bother you past sun-up, so why don't you just forget it!'

The redhead sounded agitated and walked away before Hardy could reply. He and the others — Billy Dysart, Hondo McLane, Dal Gilbert — stood there under guard, hands bound as they waited for the first show of grey light in the east.

It would be their last sunrise . . .

*   *   *

When the sun rose enough over the ravine's rim to spill a grey, amber-tinged glow down into the valley, the increasing light showed the crowd gathered around the grove of trees at the bend of the creek.

There were some fifty soldiers with Colonel O'Connor astride his buckskin stallion at their head. They were all looking towards the grove where the four rebels waited to die.

They stood on sawn-off logs, hands

bound behind their backs, knotted ropes around their necks thrown up over sturdy branches. There were birds singing in the grove, but not in the immediate vicinity of the four doomed men. They were all hatless, each having refused a blindfold.

Most of the soldiers looked impassive, a few lowered their gazes as if in shame, and a few licked their lips in anticipation of the hangings to come. A soldier stood beside each bound man, awaiting the colonel's order to kick the stumps out from under the doomed prisoners.

Their faces, too were impassive, giving no hint at what their thoughts might be. Naturally the married men, Dysart and Gilbert, were silently lamenting the loss of their families, not even having the satisfaction of knowing they would be safe and taken care of — in fact, they were tormented by the knowledge that the exact opposite would probably be the case. Hondo McLane — well, he had always been a loner, lived a rough, tough life, had sent many Yankees to meet their Maker during the war. Life hadn't appeared to hold much future for him, anyway. If it had to end here in this sweet-smelling grove with the distant sounds of birds and the sun rising, why, he could think of many worse places for a man to die.

As for Deke Hardy — a rage seethed within the man, a rage at Kyle O'Connor. If he could have just two minutes to get his hands around the man's throat, he would go to Glory a happy man, meet his Fate, spit in the Devil's eye, serve his time in Hell gladly.

But it was not to be and this was one time when he could not endure the knowledge that there was not a thing he could do about it. Hell, it hardly mattered when you got right down to it, because he had bare minutes to live . . . but, oh Lord, if he could just have those two minutes alone with O'Connor.

'Well, I trust you have all made your

peace with your Maker,' the colonel said suddenly, barely able to hide his anticipatory smile. 'I cannot allow you any more time. You understand you have committed heinous crimes against the Union and that I am quite within my rights — and *within the law* itself — in hanging you. So — ' He set his gaze on Hardy's rugged face, flinched involuntarily at the fierce hatred in the man's eyes, then raised his sword above his head.

On the down-sweep the soldiers would kick the logs from under the feet of the bound men and they would swing free, slowly strangling as the knotted rope tightened about their necks.

The sword started to descend when suddenly all heads turned at a strange sound drifting into the valley: the sound of many horses descending the trail from the world above.

All heads turned, even O'Connor's, his face darkening at the interruption — and then blanching as he saw a company of armed Union cavalry thundering down the valley towards the grove of trees.

A man in a general's uniform led them and at his side rode a civilian.

Lisa Rivera.

'Stop this immediately!' roared the stentorian-voiced general and O'Connor's men froze, their old training coming home to them hard at an order barked by a superior officer.

Kyle O'Connor's face coloured deeply and he tightened his grip on his sword, glaring at the man he now recognized as General Curtis, Chief Regulator for the District of South Missouri. He had no idea why the man was here or how he had got here, but he was damned if even the Chief Regulator was going to stop this now! *Damned if he was!*

He rammed his horse forward suddenly, scattering men, knocking down and trampling the soldier who had been standing beside Hardy, awaiting the order to kick away the tree stump. The horse slammed into Hardy, knocked him off the stump and set him swinging at the end of the rope, the hemp biting deeply into his throat and starting to strangle him.

There was uproar, but the soldiers were too disciplined to move without orders.

But Lisa Rivera was not a soldier.

She drew her small Smith & Wesson, aimed swiftly and on her second shot cut the rope through and Hardy crashed to the ground, writhing. The noose was still tight about his neck but Brick Field ran forward and yanked it loose. Hardy's breath wheezed in with a half-strangled sound and he began to cough.

O'Connor, raging, lunged his horse forward, sword swinging. Field dived aside as the blade sliced near him, then O'Connor jumped his mount around, leaned from the saddle and slashed at Hardy where he lay on the ground.

'Stop him!' roared General Curtis and Field lunged upwards and hauled the colonel out of the saddle.

O'Connor hit hard, breath gusting out of of him as the redhead wrenched the sword from his grip, then stood the man up again. O'Connor struggled free and glared wildly at his lieutenant.

'You're demoted as of now!' he snapped, but then General Curtis's horse forced between them and the general's moustache seemed to bristle as he glared down at O'Connor.

'You are not in any position to speak about *demotion*, Colonel! My God, man, I only half-believed the stories I was hearing about you, even when written complaints came in! I did not think it was possible that a Union officer could abuse his authority in such a blatant manner! Which is why I sent Mrs Rivera down here to find out just how much credence I should put in the complaints we'd received.'

Field and O'Connor both snapped their heads around to the woman who had dismounted now and was stooping over Hardy, cutting his bonds with a folding knife. She moved on to free the other three who still balanced precariously on their stumps with the nooses about their necks.

Curtis allowed himself a faint, crooked grin at O'Connor's astonishment. 'Yes, Lisa is one of our undercover agents. Internal Security, I believe is going to be the name of the department that will employ her and other suitable operatives. She came down here to put you to the test, Colonel O'Connor, and I'm ashamed to say that you failed miserably.'

The colonel swallowed, his face blotchy now, chest heaving. 'I-I acted within Reconstruction Law at all times!'

'No! You did not! If you had, I wouldn't be here now I assure you!' The general paused, drew down a deep breath. 'You are relieved from your post, Colonel, and that rank is temporary as from this moment on. You will face a court-martial for blatant breach of Reconstruction Law. There will be charges of corruption, not to mention cold-blooded murder.' The general set his hard eyes on Hardy. 'Been quite a few years, Deke.'

Hardy, rubbing his throat with the fresh ropeburn, smiled crookedly. 'Quite a few, General. You were only a colonel when I was chief scout for your company at Fort Henderson.' Hardy's voice was hoarse: it was a strain to speak.

'There were times during the war when I could've wished you were still under my command, Deke.'

Not sure if that was some kind of criticism about his sitting out the war in Idaho, Hardy stayed silent.

General Curtis, still sitting his big buckskin, turned to one of the lieutenants alongside him. 'Hec, disarm O'Connor's men and hold them in a group for questioning. No one leaves this valley without my say-so.'

While Curtis was giving detailed orders, O'Connor under the rifles of two craggy-faced troopers, Hardy moved over to Lisa Rivera.

'Reckon I owe you my life — for which I thank you.'

She shrugged elegant shoulders. 'Lucky I have been practising with my pistol.'

He grinned. 'Yeah, my luck was in today, all right, but I wouldn't've said so a couple of hours ago. How come you found this place? It's damn hard to locate unless you know it's here.'

'Brick Field had men following your friends who left town and they sent a message to him by heliograph. We had a man watching from the hills and he read the helio message, relayed it to the general who was camped in a canyon north of Springfield awaiting word from me. When we were searching for a way around the salt pans, we met the women and children who had left this valley and your sister volunteered to show us the way here.'

'Lee's all right then?'

Lisa turned and gestured. Lee was riding down the ramp from the flats above with the other women and the children, escorted by half a dozen soldiers.

'The general thought it best for them to wait in safety in case there was any more fighting.'

Hardy hurried to Lee and the other women and children ran to their husbands and fathers. Lee threw her arms about his neck.

'Thank God you're safe, Deke! I was afraid we'd be too late.'

'Almost.' He told her about Lisa Rivera shooting the rope and allowing him to fall to the ground. 'Brick Field got it off me.'

He watched her face sober abruptly at mention of the redhead's name. Frowning, he took her shoulders between his hands, looking down into her face.

'Lee, what is it about Field? I saw you before when he rescued you from that soldier. You seemed about to thank him and then — then your face just fell apart and you couldn't get away from him fast enough. What's behind that, Sis?'

She shook her head quickly, not looking at him. 'I — it's all past now. I don't think it matters any more.'

He tightened his grip on her shoulders and saw her wince but he didn't relax his hands. 'Sis, it matters! Hell, you were scared white! What the hell has he done to you?'

He glanced around and saw Field, standing with General Curtis and his officers and the crestfallen O'Connor. The redhead was only half-listening to whatever the general was saying: his attention was mainly focused on Lee Hardy. His face was set in tight lines, mouth stretched out thinly.

'What *is* it, Sis?' grated Hardy.

He could feel her trembling now and had to lean his head down to hear what she was saying. She spoke in a low quavering voice, her hands grasping his forearms now.

'I told you about that group of men who came to the house, drunk, and raped me . . . '

'Yeah, Field said all three had been found guilty, or *taken care of*, I think were his words.'

She drew down a deep breath, raising her damp eyes to his now, teeth biting lightly at her lower lip. '*Three* of them were executed. I never heard the details . . . '

He frowned. 'Yeah, that's right. All three,' he said.

She shook her head. 'There was a fourth man . . . he was never found, never identified.'

Hardy stiffened. 'Are you saying . . . ?'

'In the struggle, the fourth man held me while — well, as I fought and we stumbled around the room while they were . . . stripping me . . . I managed to get my hands on a paring knife. You know the one I mean; Ma used it, claimed it had belonged to *her* mother. The blade was worn way down from years of use and sharpening, barely an inch long.'

'Judas, Sis, I *know* the blamed knife! What about it?'

'I stabbed the fourth man with it . . . I swung it up and across my shoulder, a very awkward blow, and I just missed his throat, but the blade ripped a 'V'-shaped wound just beneath his collarbone. It didn't stop him, of course, if anything it angered him and he hit me and later — well, he was just as bad as his friends.'

'And ..?' Hardy asked tightly.

'When Field picked me up off the ground after that soldier had knocked me down, his tunic was open — I saw the wound — or the scar. Like a shallow 'V', just below his right collarbone. It — it brought everything back with a rush . . . '

Hardy still held her though not so tightly. 'Sis, you'd need to be certain-sure about this.'

'I am, Deke. But — well, it was more than a year ago. And it does seem to be finished . . . at least, I thought so . . . '

He turned away, leaving her standing, crossing to the group of officers where Field waited, watching him closely. Lisa Rivera had been watching him also, while he was speaking with his sister, her face impassive but her eyes alert.

General Curtis looked up as Hardy approached. 'Sorry to interrupt, General, but could I have a few words with Lieutenant Field?'

Curtis frowned. 'We're discussing strategy right now Hardy, it'll have to wait.'

His eyes were hard, ruthless, almost cruel.

'No, sir,' Hardy said, as the general turned back to his group and Curtis swung his head around, frowning, looking mighty annoyed.

'What was that?'

'This is important, General. It's something that's waited far too long to be settled and it has to be done now.'

Curtis continued to stare at him, then the frown eased a little as he turned to the redhead. 'You know what he's talking about, Lieutenant?'

'I think maybe I do, sir. And, he's right — it is something that should've been settled long ago. With your permission, General . . . ?'

Curtis hesitated, looking from one man to the other, then nodded curtly. 'I know you of old, Hardy — I know that look. Lieutenant Field is under open arrest, but until his part in this business is clarified, he is still an officer of the Union and therefore under my protection.'

Hardy said nothing.

Curtis shook his head slightly and gestured to Field who moved away, aware that the entire group was watching. As Hardy started to walk away, knowing Field would follow, Lisa Rivera said quietly, 'Don't do anything foolish, Mr Hardy. The general does not play favourites. If you break the law . . . '

'I know the general of old, Mrs Rivera. But I make my own law and I reckon he knows that.'

'You *are* a very stubborn man, aren't you!'

He walked on without answering and Brick Field warily followed him into the grove of trees until they were out of sight of the others and could barely hear their voices.

In a small clearing, Hardy turned to face Field and stiffened when he saw that the redhead had drawn his pistol.

'You shoot an unarmed man, I doubt the general will offer you his protection then, Brick.'

Field's face was tight, his eyes narrowed. 'She told you, didn't she? I figured it out finally, that she saw the knife scar under my collarbone earlier . . . '

'Lee told me, you lousy Yankee scum.'

'Come *on*, Hardy! You've seen how soldiers are when they win a fight, move in on a conquered town!'

'I've seen it, never took part in any of it myself and any man who does so is no more than a piece of dog's turd in my opinion.'

He thought Field would shoot him.

The man was shaking with rage at the vile insult, his knuckles about the gun butt were white, his finger tightening about the trigger, hammer cocked. A hair's more pressure and Hardy would be dead.

But Brick Field made himself relax, somehow, although his eyes were still blazing.

'By Godfrey, you take some risks, Hardy! Look, we'd bought some lousy moonshine from some of your Hardyville friends. They deliberately poisoned it, left all the fusel-oils in, added rattler venom, we found out later . . . it was *loco* booze! You must know about it!'

'Sure — about the only way they could get back at you Yankees for robbing them of their land and homes and ruining them . . . *and* their womenfolk! Even young girl children.'

'There was none of that!' Field

sounded outraged at the possibility he might be thought of as a drunken child molestor. 'We were on furlough after months without any leave. We cut loose. That damn moonshine nearly killed us. Sent us crazy! I'm not gonna say we didn't know what we were doin'. I guess we did, but after drinkin' that stuff, we just didn't *care*, Hardy! We couldn't help ourselves!'

'You're breaking my heart.'

Field's face straightened. 'All *right*! You don't wanna understand, that's too bad! But I was *ashamed*. I don't care whether you believe that or not but I was! The others figured they'd had a good time, so good it was worth the bellyache and lousy hangover where a man's eyes wanted to fall out of their sockets. They bought more of that same moonshine and aimed to go on another spree. When I couldn't talk 'em out of it, it developed into a fight and I shot one, another jumped through a window, and bled to death, and I — strung up the other. Lucky

O'Connor didn't hang *me*!'

'O'Connor has a soft spot for you.'

'Yeah, I guess that's what saved my neck. 'Course I never told him I'd been part of that rape gang. Anyway, since then, when I could, I've given your sister a break.'

'But she was still sent to that whorehouse!'

'Christ, Hardy, give *me* a break! I couldn't go agin the colonel's orders! Hell, I told you how to get her out, didn't I? I did what I could. I'm real sorry about what happened and . . . well, I guess the rest is up to you now, ain't it?'

Lisa Rivera was right: Hardy was a tough, stubborn man and he was a righteous one, too: his sister had been violated and it was his job as her only living kin to see that the matter was put right. Or as right as it could be.

That meant Brick Field had to pay for his part in harming her.

But the man held a cocked pistol pointed at his chest and he knew Field wasn't about to stand still for whatever Hardy decided to do to him.

He was gathering himself, wondering how he could possibly beat the fall of the big Remington's hammer, when there was a wild yell from beyond the grove of trees and the sound of two shots.

Then Kyle O'Connor's voice reached them, strained, with wildness, close to the limits of sanity.

'Stay back! *Back, I said*! Or I'll blow the general's brains all over this valley! If you think for one moment I'm going to be humiliated, stand trial for anything I've done to the Rebel scum in my district, you've certainly got another think coming! I only did what I saw as my duty. We don't have heroes any longer, it seems: just men who are dedicated . . . if you follow, you'll find the general dead . . . '

There were replies but Hardy didn't hear them. Field had been shaken by O'Connor's threats and his attention was diverted.

Hardy made his move. And lightning fast it was. He smashed the heel of a hand against Field's gun arm, knocking the pistol to one side. The gun went off but before the dazed redhead could bring it back, Hardy hit him on the side of the jaw, sending him stumbling. Field didn't go down all the way but staggered wildly, though still maintained his grip on the Remington. He triggered across his body and the bullet hit Hardy high in the left arm, making the limb flap violently out to one side. The impact turned him slightly so that the blow he swung missed Field by a mile. But he rammed his entire body into the lieutenant, knocking the man to his knees. Hardy brought up a knee into the middle of Field's face and snatched at the six-gun as Brick went over backwards, dazed, blood smeared across his mouth and cheeks.

Hardy missed the gun, but he leapt forward and kicked Field in the side. The man grunted and drew up his knees and there was murder in his eyes as he snapped the Remington around, hammer cocked. Hardy propped, rising to his toes, started to spin away in a desperate move.

Then O'Connor, hair awry, eyes staring fiercely, staggered into the clearing, one arm locked about General Curtis's neck.

There was blood on the general's left thigh and the leg was dragging, his weight pulling O'Connor to one side. But all that the frenzied colonel saw was Hardy and he bared his teeth as he lifted the big Dragoon pistol he had snatched from his guard before wounding Curtis and taking the man hostage.

'At least I'll finish *you!*' he gritted and Hardy started to throw himself aside as the gun blasted.

The shot was very loud in amongst the trees — and perhaps a mite *longer* than he had expected, but there was no crash of the big ball ripping the life out of him. With the impetus of his own movement, he landed on his side not far from the sprawled redhead.

O'Connor was staggering, a red streak across one side of his face, and the general tore himself free, falling. Hardy looked back to Brick Field. The man was on his side, his chest blown open by the Dragoon's ball. O'Connor must have recognized the danger from the redhead at the last second, turned the gun on him just as Field fired.

Hardy lunged forward, snatched the smoking Remington from Field's hand, rolled on to his knees as O'Connor fired the Dragoon again. The ball drove into the ground in front of Hardy as he triggered the last two shots in the six-gun.

O'Connor seemed to half-turn and fling himself away but there was no co-ordination. One half of his face was missing as he folded up into a bloody heap across the general's boots. Curtis kicked him away viciously.

Hardy turned to Field, saw the man was finished: he could see the torn heart pulsing out what was left of the man's life. Brick lifted bloody fingers and clawed at Hardy's sleeve.

'Would you have killed me?' he gasped hoarsely.

Without hesitation Hardy said, 'Yeah.'

Field seemed to give a brief nod and then slumped.

The clearing was filling rapidly with soldiers and a medico was already bending over General Curtis. Lisa Rivera came to stand by Hardy who was examining his arm wound.

'I heard what you told the redhead — you're a hard man, Deke.'

'By name and by nature,' he said flatly.

'Well you saved the general, so I imagine your troubles will soon be ironed out. He needs a man like you to convince people that Reconstruction can be a good thing.'

'I've heard it all before,' Hardy cut in. 'That's how all this started, with O'Connor telling me the same thing.'

'But General Curtis is a man of his word — I think you know that.'

Hardy nodded by way of admission.

'For a start, your land will be returned to you — I only posed as a carpetbagger to find out if all the complaints of corruption against O'Connor were true, or merely someone being vindictive. I'll move my things out as soon as possible.'

As she started to turn away, he knotted a kerchief about the wound in his arm and said, 'No hurry.'

She paused, looked at him steadily for a long minute. Then she smiled slowly.

'No — no hurry at all.'

THE END

We do hope that you have enjoyed reading this large print book.

Did you know that all of our titles are available for purchase?

We publish a wide range of high quality large print books including:
Romances, Mysteries, Classics
General Fiction
Non Fiction and Westerns

Special interest titles available in large print are:
The Little Oxford Dictionary
Music Book, Song Book
Hymn Book, Service Book

Also available from us courtesy of Oxford University Press:
Young Readers' Dictionary
(large print edition)
Young Readers' Thesaurus
(large print edition)

For further information or a free brochure, please contact us at:
Ulverscroft Large Print Books Ltd.,
The Green, Bradgate Road, Anstey,
Leicester, LE7 7FU, England.
Tel: (00 44) **0116 236 4325**
Fax: (00 44) **0116 234 0205**

Other titles in the
Linford Western Library:

THE CHISELLER

Tex Larrigan

Soon the paddle-steamer would be on its long journey down the Missouri River to St Louis. Now, all Saul Rhymer had to do was to play the last master-stroke of the evening. He looked at the mounting pile of gold and dollar bills and again at the cards in his hand. Then, looking around the table, he produced the deed to the goldmine in Montana. 'Let's play poker!' But little did he know how that journey back to St Louis would change his life so drastically.

THE ARIZONA KID

Andrew McBride

When former hired gun Calvin Taylor took the job of sheriff of Oxford County, New Mexico, it was for one reason only — to catch, or kill, the notorious Arizona Kid, and pick up the fifteen hundred dollars reward the governor had secretly offered. Taylor found himself on the trail of the infamous gang known as the Regulators, hunting down a man who'd once been his friend. The pursuit became, in every sense, a journey of death.